MIRROR
IMAGES

MADISON MURDERS - BOOK 1

By

G. A. EDWARDS

To all of my students who dream,
you inspired me to reach one of my own.

ACKNOWLEDGEMENTS

When you take forever to publish your first book, you end up with so many people you can count as blessings.

I begin with my mom who taught me to love books. This has made all of the difference in my world.

So many people read the various versions of Mirror Images and I benefited from the feedback I received from all of you. I thank Rachel, Robin, Becky, Dana, Claire, Alyssa, Jenna, Michael, and the other readers, friends, and family who answer my questions, cheer me on, and remind me not to be so hard on myself. I thank the numerous writers who have been there for me in more ways than I can list, but I do remember them.

I am grateful for the many wonderful writers, agents, and editor I've met through Romance Writers of America, Heartland Romance Authors, Mid-America Romance Authors, Society of Children's Book Writers and Illustrators. I am so happy that I actually got up the nerve to get out of my minivan and go into my first meeting of those intimidating authors who weren't so scary after all. My experience interning for New Adult Editors, Karen Grove and Nicole Steinhaus of Entangled Publishing, LLC, has also been invaluable to improve my skills.

Betty Winslow and the late C. J. Winters, my first critique partners, showed me the best groups work hard, lift you up while telling you the hard truth, and laugh together. I have been lucky to work for many years with Dyann Love Barr, Claire Ashgrove, Cathy Morrison, Judy Ridgely and Deb Sturgess as critique partners as they became the writing professionals I admire. I have been reminded about the pure joy of writing with Gemma Brocato, Lindy Dierks, Dawn Lind, Emily Swope, Edie Jo Gibson, and Diane Kratz.

Thank you to Nicole Zoltack for your earlier editing suggestions. My book became stronger with your guidance. I am grateful to author, Sherry Sirna, who offered oodles of practical advice on what to do when I got ready to publish.

I would also like to recognize Julie Rice for her art and cover design and the many things she did to help me with the author publishing process. If I was the mother of this book, Julie was the beloved aunt who dressed it up and made it pretty.

I appreciated my sister for answering my questions about Juvenile Laws.

Ryan and Michael, I'm grateful for what you both taught me about the special world of twins.

I thank my most ardent fan, Veronica Knox, for the opportunity to share the world of writing with you.

And I couldn't have accomplished this book without the unfailing support of my husband. You remain always, My Bob.

This one's harder to kill than the others. You would think a skinny little first grade girl wouldn't be so hard to drown. I mean, really! Usually I just give 'em a good crack to the head with a rock, smear a little blood on the dock or pool's edge to make it look like an accident, and roll her into the water. None of this fighting to the top stuff.

And I can't wait around forever. The sun's coming up and I need to get home before I'm missed.

Time to take the plunge.
Literally.

The Killer

Rrrrrrrrrrrrrrrrrrrrrrrrrrrrummmmmmm. Ruuuuuummmm. Putt putt putt putt.

Smack! I pitch forward and the weed trimmer goes wild.

One, two, three, FOUR! Decapitations! A floral carnage of Mrs. Bryant's prize-winning dahlias.

I straighten up, hit the kill switch, yank my earplugs out by the cord, and spin around ready to do battle with whatever unknown foe shoved me forward. All I see is my identical twin brother Max sprawling on his knees before me cradling something in his hands.

"Max, what the h…?" I reach forward to pull him up. A streak of blood marks his cheek. I jerk him the rest of the way up. How could he get blood on his face while driving a riding lawnmower? Blade's on the bottom.

"Oh crap! Max, what…" Tiny rivets of blood drip between the fingers of his cupped hands.

I unclip the weed trimmer and toss it to the side. Probably not the best idea, since it's an expensive investment for our lawn business. But panic does that. Frantic, I grab in the direction Max's hands to search for the source of the blood or possible missing digits. He leans away.

"I'm sorry, Marty. I tripped."

"Where're you hurt?" I demand, checking behind him to see if our old riding lawnmower is still upright. It is.

"It's not me, Marty."

"Let me see!" I try again to force his hands open to see the wounds. I'm only three minutes older, but I always act as if I'm the guy in charge. Usually Max allows it.

"It's not my blood. It's a baby bunny. I ran over it." He gestures with his clasped hands and a few drops of blood fling toward me.

"What?" I ask, still trying to count his fingers.

"It's the bunny. The others ran off, but..." Max's voice quavers, "I cut this one with the mower blade."

Max's dark hair, so much like my own, is plastered down on his forehead and hanging over his coffee brown eyes. It's already so steamy this morning, I'm not certain if the liquid glistening on his cheeks is sweat or tears from being soft-hearted when it comes to hurt animals.

"Crap, Max!" I draw my hands back and wipe at the drops of blood on my jeans. "A stupid rabbit? I thought you cut off your finger, or a piece of metal from the mower impaled you!" I rage with relief and repeat. "Crap!"

Usually I am pretty easy-going, but fear brings out my mean side.

Max waits until I get control of myself. After fifteen and a half years as brothers, he knows I bluster when I get agitated. Then he says softly, "There's a big cut on its side, Marty."

Max peers fretfully down at his cupped hands. He opens them enough I can see the bunny's tiny face peeking out even as its blood drips to the ground. With its body shuddering in starts and stops, this panting bunny is the definition of pitiful.

I soften. "He's awfully small. He probably won't make it."

"I know." Max sucks in a ragged breath and gives me a look of hope. You know the kind. It's the one that puppies and little kids give someone when they believe you are just the person to make their dreams come true. The look that always makes my chest ache, because I've learned that the world isn't all happy smiles, bright sunshine, or getting to use an action replay in all of your favorite video games. Too many bad things have happened to good people. Like our dad.

"Do you think if I take him over to Dr. Grimaldi, that he can stitch him up?"

This is Max at his essence. Always willing to help out. You would think since my twin and I began in the same egg sac and our DNA lined up in genetic perfection that our personalities would be the same. We do have the similar facial features, tall, rangy builds, and the voices that sound alike that people expect from identical twins. But our personalities, not so much.

It isn't that I'm the heartless twin or anything, but I worry more about practical issues of our health and survival. Like always making sure Max is okay. Or how much money we won't be making if all of the yard work isn't done before the Garden Club ladies show up at 11:00.

There aren't that many job opportunities in a small town for two teenage guys that aren't old enough to drive. With our dad dead, our family struggles on just one income. We don't need an injured bunny to cause our mowing and trimming business, Twin Cuts, to get a reputation for being unreliable. Both of us are setting aside enough money to buy insurance when we get our licenses next spring. I also have it in my mind to put aside some cash toward future college costs.

But I care more about Max and his healthy state of mind than cash, cars, or college. It may cause a time crunch to get our work completed on time, but Operation: Save the Bunny is a go.

Sometimes it plain sucks to be the responsible one in the Jamison twindom.

"Just go. But get back here as quickly as you can," I sigh and add, "I mean that. You have to hurry this time."

Max nods and then carefully lopes off toward the vet's office a couple of blocks away. Nobody there will be surprised to see Max show up with an injured animal. He'd been like a magnet for them ever since we were kids. Being fifteen and a few months hasn't changed Max's soft heart, or need to help others of all species.

I turn and pick up the weed trimmer to inspect it for damage. It's fine, but the topped flower heads need to be taken to the mulch bucket on the cart we tow behind the mower. Reaching the cart, I set the weed trimmer down, toss the flowers, and stretch the bottom of my shirt up to mop at the sweat covering my face. A quick sniff to my underarms confirms I smell rank. Nothing I can do about that now, so I grab my water jug. I swish the cool water around in my mouth, spit, then drink deeply.

Only nine in the morning and already scorching. That's Missouri in late July. Hot, humid, and hotter than the other "h" word not fit for polite company. Ever wondered if the old cliché of it being so hot outside you can fry an egg on the pavement is a real possibility? It is, on days like today when it's above one hundred degrees even in the shade. My friend Billy did it in fifth grade. He ate it, too. At least when school starts in a few weeks, I'll be able to watch classmates eating nasty things in the nice cool air-conditioned cafeteria.

Break almost over, I put my sunglasses back on and peer around the Bryant's property. It is a nice one. Really nice. The big house is surrounded by other big houses and sits on a small lake dotted with personal docks, holding boats or wave runners or both. Way out of my family's lower middle class income range.

I smile when I look across the lawn next door. Some college-aged guy hobbles bare-footed toward the long ramp leading to the swimming dock. His shorts hang well below his waist, his hair is sticking up all over, and he's holding his head up at a weird angle like it weighs too much. I'll go out on limb and guess Hangover Guy somehow hopes a dip in the lake will give him some relief. I sigh again, wishing I had time for a quick swim. A night spent swimming and partying with friends might be good too.

The person I would really like to enjoy some time with is Kayla Gallagher. Normally my best friend and I spend most of our summer afternoons hanging out at the public beach on the other side of the lake. But this year I have the mowing jobs and she's busy at the community's activity center teaching crafts to kids. I can always count on Kayla to be fun, loyal, and not afraid to punch me in the arm when I say something jerky. I miss her. Probably more than I should miss someone I say is just a friend.

Smack! I swat impatiently at a tiny sweat bee that has taken advantage of my brief break to sting my forearm. Better get moving. I shove in my earplugs, rev up the weed eater and try to get my mind off the only thing that heats me up more than hard work in the summer sun. Kayla.

Mother Nature's giving it her best to be the hottest thing this summer. But the truth is, she's got nothing in her weather arsenal to compare to the heat generated by the sight of Kayla in a bikini.

Maybe it's the earplugs or my preoccupation with someone's swimwear that prevents me from hearing Hangover Guy's screams for help a few minutes later. But it's the blowing dust from police cars and an oncoming sporadic, piercing whine of the ambulance that are my first clues to a problem next door. Before I can get around the corner of the house to get a closer look at the dock where the action seems to be, I notice Max running full-out across the lawn toward me. Is he trying for a heart attack in this heat?

He comes in for an awkward stop, gasps, then asks, "Are you okay?" He flings his hair out of his eyes and looks me over. "The sirens…"

"I'm fine. Take a breath, Bro." I wait for the American Beauty Rose red color on his face to turn to the softer

Compassion variety's shade. I've been reading the little labeling tags in the rose beds while I work.

"I thought you needed help."

"It's next door. Come on. Let's go see what's going on."

We turn and walk closer. Nope, no police bust of any kind to observe, but there's something. Something bad enough to make me wish I hadn't left my house this morning.

Hangover Guy from next door found something floating in the lake. A someone.

And while it's still possible Max's mission to save the bunny may succeed, Hangover Guy's Operation: Save the Drowning Girl?

It's a failure from the get-go. She's dead.

I know Mom and Dad think it will help me cope better if I talk with you. I really don't see how you can help me, but it's better than trying to drink myself into oblivion.

Anyway, the day before what happened was great. Folks were out of town and frat brothers were down to party on the lake.

I drank a lot of cold ones, so my head was poundin' next morning. Figured a quick swim might clear it up. Got near the end of the dock and saw something bobbing on the surface. It was a big bow. Like on some kind of present, but this one was attached to the little girl's ponytail.

You know what I'm having the hardest time with?

The crunch. You know, when her chest broke in from my hands pushing down so hard during CPR. Nothing can prepare you for...for feeling that give in under your hands.

It just sucks. I mean, the whole thing really just sucks.

Jason Horning a.k.a Hangover Guy

Morning bus rides are predictable. You can count on the drone of the bus motor, the roar of multiple tires on the pavement, loud music screeching through scratchy cheap speakers, the wind smacking you in the face from open windows, and the high pitched voices of little kids. All of these sounds are present on the first day of my sophomore year, too. Only today, hearing those little kids so excited about coming to school just reminds me of the dead one who is not.

Natalee Peterson.

I know her. Well, knew her. Her brother Jacob has been my brother's best friend since grade school. Max and I have been hanging around her house with Jacob since before she was even born. To compare with the other seven year old girls, she was tiny for her age, but tough. Probably from trying to keep up with all of the older boys. "General Natalee" was our nickname for her, because she wanted to be the boss of everyone. She wore these big, puffy bows on top of her head, and it wasn't nice, but we all took great joy smashing them flat when she got on our nerves.

Natalee's funeral had been the first one Max and I attended since our dad died. I think this one was even worse. With Dad we were too young to really get the concept of death. Now we understand how permanent it is all too well. I know that as soon as our car got close to the packed funeral home for the service, my chest tightened and I felt like I couldn't breathe. It reminded me of nearly eight years ago at the graveyard when I realized my dad was going into the ground for good. I could tell when I looked over at Mom's clenched jaw and Max's white pallor that they didn't feel any better about the situation than I did.

The scene outside the funeral home that day's crazy. The parking lot's so full Mom has to park around the corner. Then there's such a long line of mourners and it's so hot outside that an ambulance crew's already working with a couple of people who passed out. A news crew from the city is set up at the edge of the street and tries to interview friends and family.

The worst moment comes when the blonde reporter from Channel Six corners Hangover Guy, who the paper says is really Jason Horning. I don't know what she says to him, but he looks like he wants to hurl his breakfast or punch her in the head. I want to punch that reporter in for upsetting the poor guy. Death is hard enough without people adding to the pain.

Whack!

Ow. My attention rushes back from my thoughts of death to the bus ride, thanks to a kick from my buddy Ray O'Rear. He grins from his seat across the aisle.

"Heads up, Marty, we're here! First day of high school." He stands and leans out the bus window announcing, "All you fine ladies, behold. The mightiest young stud of

Madison High School, Home of the Mighty Mules, has arrived."

I roll my eyes and think I might be the one to hurl from his words. "Ray, all we're doing is crossing the parking lot. The middle school is right over there." Our school is unique in the area because it only has grades ten through twelve, rather than the normal four. Nothing innovative about why. The building could only hold three grades.

Ray snorts. "Marty, my man. We're sophomores now. It's a whole new world of cougary juniors and senior hotties. I'm gonna find one with her own car to drive me around in style."

My friend is convinced he is Madison's answer to a lady-loving street thug. Sporting the fiery red hair and the skinny build of a baseball player, he's not either of these things. But he's a good guy and I admire him for thinking he could be.

"You can drive yourself in a few months. Besides, any girl with a car'll want to run you over, not drive you around."

"Don't be hatin' on my master plan. Better turn around and get your brother. Don't want him to wake up in the bus lot again. Later, man." Ray joins the line of those waiting to exit.

"Later."

I turn to view the seat behind me. Max is asleep. Again. I sigh. I had some hope I wouldn't have to be responsible this year to wake him up and remind him to get off the bus. Once in grade school when I stayed home sick the substitute bus driver hadn't done the legally required seat check before exiting. Max woke up an hour later alone in the locked bus in the district's parking lot. A mechanic finally heard Max beating on the windows and yelling for help and helped him get out. Results of that morning? Brother traumatized. Mom irate. Substitute driver fired.

"Max." Nothing. " Max, you gotta wake up."

Most people can't sleep on a noisy bus, but Max's bipolar meds make it difficult for him to stay awake in the mornings. In the genetic lottery for being B. P., my dad was, Max is, and Mom and I are not. More proof that same parents, womb, environment, and even exact same DNA won't produce identical, physical, or emotional beings.

It seems like that these days everyone claims to understand everything about being bipolar from watching all those psychological dramas at the movies. I get frustrated with uninformed people who think everyone who is B.P. hears voices or becomes violent. Wrong. After the amount of counseling our whole family has been through together, we are all nearly experts on the subject. Basically, bipolar is a chemical imbalance that affects mood. It can't be fixed, but most people can manage the highs and lows with medication. Especially with family support. There are people who commit illegal acts due to problems with a diagnosed mental disorder, but many people cope well and live safely among the rest of society's so-called normal people.

Refusing his meds and help from the family is why Dad ended up like he did. Bipolar affects people differently. Our father was the severe depression type. Max usually goes to the other end of the spectrum of behaviors. He suddenly has tons of excess energy and talks faster than normal before getting too hyper to sleep. Mom became a nurse a few years ago, so now she's extremely proactive about

Max's medical care. We call her the *Pill Nazi*. She says that having been married to a man who refused treatment and then committed suicide qualifies her to be one, and to deal with it. Even though it can be a pain for everyone, Mom and I both agree that some extra effort on our parts and Max having to deal with some morning medication grogginess is a small price to pay for his overall mental health.

Duane, our bus driver, reaches over to turn down the radio blaring out country songs and stops high-fiving the kids exiting to bellow from the front of the bus, "Hurry up, Jamisons. I got another load to pick for the elementary."

I stand, grab my backpack, and lean over to nudge my brother's shoulder. "Max, get up. We're here. Get your stuff."

Max sits up slowly, blinking. His eyes are bleary and unfocused and I feel bad about having to wake him. He's been groggier than normal since Natalee was found. Grief for her, worry about his friend Jacob, and the residual emotional effects of our dad's suicide aren't a good mix of emotions for anyone's mental health. Especially someone like Max, who is so focused on helping others.

I ask, "Still got your schedule and locker combination in your backpack pocket?"

Enough people have exited the bus now to hear the *unzip* and *zip* as he checks.

"Yeah. It's all here."

"Okay, let's go." Starting down the aisle I add over my shoulder, "Remember, if you have a problem, the new counselor said to go to his office." The new guy we met at orientation seems nice enough.

"*O-kay!* Smarty Marty. I got this." Max's sarcasm is apparent.

"Somebody has to keep you in line, Laxy Maxy!" I counter and pause just enough to let him bump into my backpack. Take that, brother.

Our old nicknames aren't too p.c., because they're true. Our school performance is one area where everyone can tell us apart. I do better in academics and take the more advanced classes. Max doesn't. He isn't lazy. He gets his assignments completed, but his work ethic is much more relaxed and he isn't as quick to get concepts.

Smarty Marty is better than the Farty Marty that Max used to call me. I'll admit that one is still kind of true sometimes.

Once off the bus, my brother and I stop to study the large number of students in front of the school. Max spots Jacob across the lawn and mutters a goodbye before heading over. Usually at this point I would find Kayla, but she had early dance team practice. So when I see a couple of guys from last year's advanced math class wave at me, I walk over to catch up.

It is such a normal beginning to the school year that I am surprised when a fight breaks out. I am even more surprised to be an active participant in it.

So many people at the funeral came up to the front and shared. Just had to tell everyone how much they loved Natalee and how they wished they could have done more for her. Hypocrites.

Where was everyone when Natalee needed someone? Did they listen to her problems? Did they try to help? No!

But I listened. And I helped.

The Killer

3

"Stop it, Max! I mean it." Spitting blood, I use my tongue to check if all of my teeth are still in my mouth. They are, but two feel loose. Squeezing my arm tighter in the headlock on Max, I try to dodge more blows from his fists. "Cool it. You're goin' to get in more trou—" *Whuff!* I take a hard elbow to my ribs.

"Let! Me! Go!" Max enunciates with purpose. Cries of *Fight! Fight! Fight!* echo around us from the bystanders circling our group. At this point the only fight going on is me trying to keep Max from getting away to punch some upperclassman. I have no idea who the guy is or what horrible act he could've committed to motivate Max to be shoving, cursing, and trying to egg him on to take the first punch. Heck, Max and I only got off the bus two or three minutes earlier. Now, I'm doing my best to keep Max from inflicting or receiving further injuries. Max, however, is doing his best to get free by causing me multiple injuries.

Thunk. Max lands his fist on my forehead. Ow! Who knew that whole seeing stars idea was real?

"Stop it! Max, don't make me hurt you."

"Like you even can, Marty." Max throws up his fists at my face again.

MIRROR IMAGES

A distinct disadvantage when attempting to forcibly subdue your identical twin is you're too close in size and body type to achieve a clear advantage. Being mirror image twins means we're alike, but opposite-handed. I use my right hand to apply the most pressure to the headlock. Max uses his left to swing with intense dedication at my face. Neither of us is gaining control of the other until Max changes his strategy. He suddenly drops his full weight and we hit the ground.

"Get up!" I scream in Max's ear and try to gain enough footing to drag him upright. "Quit it now. Stop it!" I squeeze even harder and increase my chokehold efforts.

Once I finally get some traction and we're up again, I demand. "What is wrong with you?" I shake him as best as I can while both of his hands wrap around my arm and tug, trying to break my hold.

"Nobody's gonna talk like that to my friend. Marty, let me go or I'm goin' to kick your puny little a—"

Although I have a good idea of what Max intends to say next, I never hear it. Our brother-on-brother combat prevents us from hearing when other students change their chants of *Fight* to *Security*. What we both do notice very quickly is just how solid the front lawn of the school feels when we are ripped apart and our faces slam down on it.

There's a piece of important information I don't recall being covered at last week's high school orientation.

Jacob. That's who motivated Max to get mad enough to cuss, shove, and try to fight the other guy. Turns out I am the only one he got to punch multiple times. Lucky me.

At least, that's what I think from overhearing some of the testimony of a parade of witnesses who have been through the office. They seem to agree that the upper-classman began needling Jacob about Natalee's death just as Max showed up. Words were exchanged and then Max went ballistic and began shoving. I'm proud Max's a stand-up guy and willing to stand up for his friend, but I really hope both of us won't be kicked out of school for his loyalty.

"Madison High School, Home of the Mighty Mules, how may I direct your call?" the receptionist answers as I sit just outside of the office of Principal Hershel Morris awaiting my fate. Max will most likely join me here if they ever let him out of the nurse's office.

"Yes, Mrs. Jamison, let me transfer you."

Great, my mom is on the phone with my new principal. I don't even need to hear Mom's actual responses to know how this is going to go. First, she'll freak out about getting a call from the school. Next, she'll freak out that there was a fight with injuries. The final and biggest freak-out of all will occur when she learns both of her sons are involved.

"Mrs. Jamison. This is, uh, Principal Hershel Morris over at the, uh, high school? I apologize for contacting you at work, but we have had, uh, phy, phyci, a fight involving your sons, uh, Max, uh, Maxwell and, uh, Martin."

Try using Max and Marty, Mr. Administrator. I still haven't officially met him, but it is clear that multiple syllabic names are only one of his numerous potential verbal downfalls.

"Well, they both have some injuries. Yes, we are, uh, sure it was both of …"

Hopefully, Principal Morris is the forgiving type. I know that when I get called in, the sight of my puffy lip isn't going to make the best first impression. Surely he'll appreciate that the lip and other bruises came from my attempt to break up the fight, rather than to instigate one. One thing I do remember from the high school orientation is that the first person to throw a punch is automatically suspended. That would be Max. My lip is the result.

Where is my brother, anyway? I shift in my chair and stare at the door where the nurse took him. I don't want to admit it, but I take care of him too often not to worry that his injuries may be worse than I thought. What if the nurse turned him over to cops? Or Juvie came to pick him up instead? He could be in jail or lockup or something. Mom isn't the only family member freaking out now.

"Young man. Young Man!"

It takes me a minute to realize I am the young man being addressed by the frowning receptionist.

"Please come here and get this waste receptacle," she demands. "You're making a terrible mess on the floor."

I look down. The ice bag I have been holding to my lip is dripping on the hardwood floor. She shoves a trashcan toward me.

"Be certain you keep the drips in that can. The custodian doesn't need any extra work."

"Yes, ma'am. Thank you, ma'am."

She just glares at my attempt to suck up. I'm not normally one of those guys, but I'm willing to try anything at this point to get in good with someone. I can tell I will need someone on my side as Principal Morris continues his side of the conversation.

"Yes Mrs. Jamison, I understand this, uh, type of behavior is not typical of Max. I do understand he is bipolar. But even if recent medication changes may have affected his behavior, Mrs., uh, Jamison..." The principal sounds like Max and I do trying to argue against Mom when she gets on a roll. *Out of his element*. Usually the nicest, polite lady in the world, my mom becomes quite persistent if the subject concerns something or someone she cares about.

"—regardless of his medication issues, we here at, uh, Madison High School have to be consistent in upholding the school's discipline procedures. Max came up with no prov, uh, provica, uh, warning and violently attacked the other boy."

Violently attacked? Since when did a couple of shoves become a *violent attack*? Maybe my brother should have punched that guy after all. This principal jerk makes it sound like this morning was a wild animal or some kind of flesh eating zombie attack! It was a couple of shoves. It isn't like Max jumped the guy and tried to eat his face off. Middle school dodge ball is an example of a violent attack and the school still allows it. Next Principal Jerkface'll suggest Max needs to be contained or schooled separately from general population. That's against the law. So my brother shoved a guy to defend his friend—it's a good thing, right?

"Ma'am, district policy requires, uh, minimum two day suspension for Maxwell. We'll count the rest, uh, of today as the first day. As for Martin, we believe he, uh, was only trying to restrain, uh, his brother and will receive no consequences."

Yes! No suspension for this guy. I grin widely with relief until my split lip reminds me why this is a bad idea. Then a door opens and the school nurse ushers Max inside and all thoughts of rejoicing end when Max raises his head. I can't help the inappropriate exclamation I make under my breath.

So much for us being identical twins. Post fight, I have a split lip and a scrape on my cheek. Max is barely recognizable. You can tell he fought back after getting put down to the pavement. One eye is deeply purpled and puffy. He's got scrapes all over his cheeks and one side of his face is swollen and misshapen. Even the collar of his shirt is ripped and that allows me to see the numerous bruises covering his throat. The air sucks out of my chest and I can feel bile surge up my throat when I realize I did that part of the damage to him.

I open my mouth to apologize until I remember one important thing.

Everything that's happened this morning is his fault. The fight, the bruises, and this trip to the office before any classes began.

The bag of ice lands on the floor with a slushy thump. It lies forgotten while my mind and body war to determine whether the feelings of relief that Max is not in jail or the hospital will win over my strong urge to pound on him. I flex the fingers on my hands together in an attempt to prevent me from making them into fists. My hands, one chilled from the icepack and the other hot with my rage, the perfect metaphors for my feelings. Cool reason says forgive him. Hot rage says clobber him. Still royally ticked off, I squeeze harder until my knuckles turn white and wait for the rage to begin to recede.

Finally, since I doubt Principal Morris will be too forgiving of the Jamison twins being in a fight twice before ten a.m., I gain control of my rage, release my fingers, and bend over to clumsily pick up the bag of ice. I try to glare at Max, but it's a waste of my time. He can barely see out of the one eye and the other is mostly covered by his hanging hair.

After a few minutes of silence, except for the continual drip of the leaking icepack, Max whispers, "You getting suspended too?"

I ignore him for as long as I can. "I don't think so. You're gone for two days starting now." I motion toward Principal Morris's door. I can't hear any talking in his office, so I figure he's off the phone and Mom is on her way.

"Oh." Max takes a shuddering breath that tells me he is pretty close to giving up all pretense of holding it together. "I am sorry, Marty. I didn't want you to get hurt or in trouble."

I wait a few seconds before sighing and replying, "Whatever."

"I thought Jacob needed my help, because..." Max adds after a moment, "he's having such a hard time."

"Of course he's having a hard time. His sister is dead. But Max, you can't always be...," I begin.

"He keeps blaming himself for not taking Natalee swimming more often. He thinks she wouldn't have gone to the lake alone if he had." Max looks over at me and the word *stricken* pops into my head. "What if he's right?"

"He doesn't know that, Max. Nobody really ever knows why some people choose to do stuff that makes them die."

We lapse into silence again.

"Mom is going to be so…," Max shakes his head, unable to finish his thought. So I do it for him. All is not forgiven, after all.

"I predict livid, disappointed, and definitely in a grounding mood. Say goodbye to personal freedom and use of all game systems."

"That's just great." My brother broods, then uses his good hand to indicate the dripping ice bag. "Your mouth okay?"

"Yeah, a couple of my teeth're loose." I run my tongue over them again. Ouch! Still there.

"So, I guess I pack a pretty good punch for a little brother, huh?" He attempts a rueful smile.

Is it too late to hit him?

"Too soon for joking, *little* brother," I warn. After a moment, I sit back in my chair and gesture with my free hand to his injuries. "Whadda bout you? You okay?"

"I guess. Face and throat hurt. Nurse said I've got a bunch of bruises. See." He lifts his head to better let me view his neck area.

They're bad. And I put them there.

So Max and I might not have that freaky twins who feel each other's pain connection like they talk about on those weird TV shows, but seeing him bruised and knowing I caused them makes my own throat feel like I can't swallow. Or it could be simply guilt that is choking me up.

"I know. I put those there." Maybe humor is the way to go, but I still wince when I lift the corner of my mouth to add, "Guess I'm one strong *older* brother."

Max sits in silence until what I said sinks in and then he snorts. We smile as best as we're able. Then Principal Morris calls out for both of us to, uh, join him in his, uh, office.

Not too sure what is louder—the clunk of the icebag hitting the bottom of the trashcan or the clunk of my heart dropping somewhere near my intestines.

I feel so bad for the Petersons. We used to be neighbors when the girls were babies, and our families have always kept in touch.

Now I worry whether Robin and Shane are going to make it through this together. Even before Natalee's accident, they were seeing a marriage counselor. I just don't know. And poor Jacob. Losing Natalee is just so hard on everyone.

My husband and I struggle with how to comfort our daughter. None of our parenting books cover how to help a child her age grieve. Before this, Lexi's only experience with death was her turtle, Princess Peasblossom. That's been two years ago and sometimes she still gets weepy about it at bedtime.

I've heard the activity center is going to offer some peer counseling. I hope so. Maybe the older kids can help the little ones deal with this.

Mother of Alexa Gover

"Scan your card please."

I fish my new student I.D. out of my pocket to run through the automated lunch system. I try to smile and even though it has been a whole day since the fighting, my mouth is sore enough that it's more of grimace.

The hair-netted lunch lady doesn't appear to notice anything as she responds in the monotone of someone who says the same few words hundreds of times a day. "Thank you. Next."

I pocket my card and move on to grab utensils and tray. Choice-A, mushy pasta, looks to be a softer and a better choice than Choice-B, crunchy tacos. After grabbing a scoop, I check out the extras while inwardly debating who I might find to sit with. The principal was sure to stress the need for me to stay out of trouble. I have been careful to stay out of the path of anyone seeking revenge for Max shoving them. I doubt I'll get a chance to say that I'm the other twin.

When I feel a tap on my shoulder I nearly drop my tray. I turn, poised to employ a fight-or-flight response based on the size of my potential opponent.

grins mockingly at me. "Dude, you about tossed cookies."

"Not cool. And *tossing* one of those pieces of granite is about all I might manage today. My teeth're still too loose to chew those things."

"Whatcha ya so nervous about? Fraid you're gonna get in a fight?" Ray rags.

"Been there. Done that. Just trying to make it through a day without a repeat." I pick up a couple of yogurts and a banana. Nice, soft textures. Sore mouth or not, a guy has to eat.

"Max ready to come back tomorrow?" Ray asks, snagging two apples and a bag of chips.

I don't say anything about the amount of food Ray is adding to his tray and he extends the same favor to me. Ray's dad has been out of work for over a year, so we both now qualify for fee reduced meals. We don't talk about it. Got to honor the guy code and ignore the bad stuff.

"You know, Marty, I would've had y'all's back and everything yesterday, but I was already in the senior's hall getting with a couple of cheerleaders. We had a little business, if you know what I mean." That's Ray Speak for trying to get the girls to notice him by any means possible. Ray hasn't hit his growth spurt yet and girls in high school tend to overlook him in more than one way.

"Where you want to sit?" I ask, pausing to look over the cafeteria.

"Marty. Marty! Over here!"

Kayla Marie Gallager, my smart, pretty, *just friends* friend beckons me over to her table. Yesterday we didn't have the same lunch shift, so we couldn't eat together. I don't want to miss our first real chance to hang out together.

I look over at Ray. He shrugs before waggling his eyebrows and heads off to another table.

I smile and stride toward Kayla. Finally. Something great about this week to enjoy.

"Hey," I say, setting my tray down and folding my legs into the bench seat.

"Hey back." She studies the damage on my face, "You doing okay?"

"Mostly. Max looks a lot worse than I do."

"Oh."

"Enjoying the school's rabbit food?" I motion toward her plate of healthier lunch options from the salad bar.

"Hardly. I don't know how the lettuce can be so limp on the second day of school." She points with a carrot stick. "Your pasta looks like one of the seven gross wonders of the world."

"Wouldn't you hate to see the other six?" I say before digging into it anyway.

"I don't understand how you can eat something that smells like wet socks." Kayla wrinkles her nose while crunching her carrot.

"Maybe I need it to maintain my fabulous physique," I joke. I resemble a tall, animated stick figure, so Kayla simply rolls her eyes and moves on.

"How have your classes been?"

"Algebra II was okay. Mostly review. Science has some old hippie guy for a teacher, but kind of cool. He's big into everyone doing their part to save the environment. He wants everyone to sign up for a stream clean team."

"Did you?" she asks.

"I put my name under the *Interested but not yet Committed* heading. He's supposed to give us more information."

"You have to promise me you won't do it."

I swallow my pasta slowly to cover my surprise at Kayla's reaction. She's usually like Max when it comes to helping others and is first to volunteer for causes. It's how she got the summer job at the recreation center.

She sees my puzzled expression and takes a deep breath before indicating my injured mouth adding, "With your kind of luck there could be a flash flood or something. You might end up down creek in mud up to your neck. You bruise easily." She manages a small smile while pointing toward my face.

I'm not buying her attempt at levity. She seems really upset. She knew Natalee too and any mention of water probably reminds her of the drowning. Any mention of a little girl dying must remind Kayla of her younger sister's death years ago.

I go all male, ignore her comments, and deflect by asking, "How were your classes?"

Kayla still looks troubled, but she plays the game. "They're okay, except for Phys-Ed. Remember in eighth grade when we studied about those evil female prison guards?"

I nod, unsure of where she is going with this question.

"Well, I think this teacher is a direct descendant." Kayla nods to convince me. "I may have a former German war criminal for a teacher."

"Really?" I tease, grateful for a less personal topic. "Is she dressed in uniform and carries a whip? That would be cool."

Kayla throws her carrot stick at me. "Now you sound like Ray. There's no whip that I know of, but her last name is Fritz and I hear she drives a Volkswagen."

"Zen eat up, my friend. You vill need fortitude to survive da Fraulein."

"I'm not certain if I should chide you for being socially inappropriate or simply report you for such a bad fake German accent," inserts Mrs. Wheaten.

Kayla and I turn around to reply at the same time to our favorite middle school employee, our former counselor.

"Sorry, I was just kidding Kayla about her P.E. teacher," I shrug.

"Hi, Mrs. Wheaten!"

"It's good to see both of you." Mrs. Wheaten sits down sideways on the bench next to Kayla and across from me. "So, how were your summers?"

Mrs. Wheaten's the kind of adult we didn't mind telling stuff. She's not judgmental or preachy.

"It was great," Kayla says. "I did the Arts and Crafts Day Camp you helped me arrange."

"I thought you would like it. Marty, what did you and Max accomplish this summer?"

"Mostly we just hung out and mowed yards for people."

"It must have been good for you, because you're tan and you look like you've possibly grown a few inches," she compliments, being wise enough to know every teen male wants to hear that.

"Thanks Mrs. Wheaten." I sit up straight on the bench.

"How are your classes so far?"

Kayla answers first, "Pretty good. But my new gym teacher is..."

"...Coach Fritz," Mrs. Wheaten finishes. "That explains Marty's botched attempt at a German accent. I've been on a couple of district committees with her, and Eva is quite a nice person." Mrs. Wheaten chuckles at Kayla's look of disbelief. "Other students have told me that with her leadership for motivation, you will end the year in the best physical condition of your life."

Kayla's moan is audible even over all of the noise in the cafeteria.

"Marty, I heard you and Max ran into a problem earlier. Are you doing okay?" Mrs. Wheaten looks into my eyes.

I swallow, "That mostly involved Max. I am fine."

"Yeah, Marty was the good guy." Kayla complimenting me is good. I smile. Ouch.

Mrs. Wheaten reaches out and pats my forearm, "It's was nice of you to choose to help Max out in this instance."

"I guess," I mumble. From our previous discussions in her office, Mrs. Wheaten knows I sometimes consider that feeling of being responsible for Max to be a burden.

"Well, I must get back over to the middle school to help the sixth graders try to remember their locker combinations." She sighs dramatically. "Tom, the custodian, is already threatening to quit if they all don't learn them before the end of the week."

Kayla and I laugh. Tom threatens to quit every year when students don't bother to learn their combinations. Always claims all those kids needing help between every hour are going to wear him and his master key out.

"Kayla, before I go I wanted to talk to you privately about the possibility of another volunteer opportunity. Do you have a minute?" Mrs. Wheaten asks.

"Sure."

"Have a good rest of the week, and year, Marty. Come see me sometime," Mrs. Wheaten says over her shoulder as she and Kayla head out to the hall where it is much quieter.

I focus on shoveling in as much food as I can with my tender mouth until Kayla returns. She looks pensive and I wonder what Mrs. Wheaten wants.

"It was great to see Mrs. Wheaten," I venture.

"Yes. I'm going to miss talking with her so much this year," Kayla agrees distractedly. "She wants to know if I will be on the peer mentoring committee for elementary students. The ones who were friends with Natalee. She thinks I could help them with managing their grief."

"Because Krista died from a seizure when you both were young, right?"

"That's what the autopsy report said." Kayla's hand moves up to smooth her hair and adjust her bow. It's her sign that she's uncomfortable with this subject.

"What did you say?"

"I told her I would think about it. With all that happened in my family after my sister died, I don't know how good of an example we are at managing grief."

She has a point. Krista's death tore their family up. It's what caused her mom to start drinking and why her dad just up and left one day. Nobody knew his whereabouts for over a year until the phone call came explaining he died in a fall on some overseas worksite. That news sent her mom, Cindy, on a bender so intense she ended up in a treatment facility for months.

"You seem like you have yourself together," I state loyally. "That's probably why Mrs. Wheaten thought to ask you."

She did have herself together. A lot of that could be attributed to her aunt. Once Cindy was hospitalized, Susan stepped in and took custody of Kayla. She quit her job as a traveling engineer and opened her own construction company to provide income and some stability. She still did some summer jobs out of town and took Kayla with her until this one, but now the whole family lives in a new duplex across town. Susan lives on one side, Cindy on the other when she is able, and Kayla goes between them as needed. We actually met their family years ago when one of Susan's workers recommended Mom to provide afterschool care. Mom and Susan became best friends, so we even do some of the holidays together.

"I guess." Kayla toys with her napkin twisting and shredding it.

"I think you have a lot to offer people. I want to spend time with you."

Before I realize what I'm doing I reach across the table to still her hand. An act that could fall under the *just friends* relationship guidelines, but we forget to let go until the bell rings and we have to take our trays up. Then we grab each other's hands on the way to our next class. Just like that, our just friends status changes.

It's not easy to pick the ones who need my help the most. So many of the girls have families who don't treat them right. Some of them get hit or touched in the bad way or their parents fight or it's just that nobody cares enough to pay attention to them.

Natalee isn't the first one I ever helped. You would think someone would pay enough attention to notice that. They might figure out the person helping all these girls is me. Or would it be I?

Grammar doesn't matter too much in this situation.

The Killer

"All of you are in this newspaper class because your ninth grade English teacher thought you could be a good staff member. Please remember it is a privilege to represent Madison High and write articles and take photos. Your school depends on you."

Our Print Media I teacher/newspaper sponsor, Miss Brandel, continues listing the attributes of a good member of the class. I can tell she's trying to sound like she can handle being in charge. I really think she's the new young teacher who got volunteered for the job and doesn't know how much work goes into sponsoring the newspaper.

Last year during enrollment when I heard about the possibility of being on the newspaper staff, I hadn't been sure I wanted to do it, but it sounded better than the other English curriculum. Those classes start the year by reading *Julius Caesar* aloud. I don't mind the play so much and will read it later this year, but hearing some sophomores verbally assassinate the Bard's text is a true definition of a tragedy.

Miss Brandel continues, "Since the class has already watched the History of the Press documentary and finished your preliminary writing assessments, it is time for me to learn more about each of you. This will aid me in…"

I only halfway listen. Instead I do what I have been doing for over a week now. Grin inanely over at Kayla who's seating with me at our worktable. It's embarrassing how much I like her.

Miss Brandel continues, "This survey will aid me in matching the most qualified writer to cover each topic. Questions? Yes?"

"Miss Brandel, I just want to write about sports. Me and Jeff could cover all the games. We're on the team."

Billy makes it sound like they're gods and expects everyone to bow down.

"Maybe your partner Jeff will have some ideas to broaden your interests," suggests Miss Brandel.

"Planes. I like them and I want to be in the Air Force," Jeff offers.

"Commendable goal. Do you know much about aviation?"

"Some." Jeff grins. "My mom says I've been trying to fly since I was a kid. Once I actually put on a red cape and jumped right off the roof of my grandma's porch."

Students snicker.

"Way to go, Icarus," a girl named Claire calls out.

Most of the class laughs. Kayla rolls her eyes in derision. She claims she doesn't like Claire due to her artsy style of clothing and wry humorous remarks, but I think her dislike is mostly due to jealousy. I made the mistake of telling Kayla that Claire and I are project partners in advanced math this year and how much fun we're going to have working together. It's stupid for Kayla to be threatened. She's the girl I want. But I wouldn't like it either if I thought Kayla was having a good time in a class with another guy.

When Claire adds, "So what were the results of your attempted lift-off, Jeff?" I want to hear the answer like everyone else in class, but I just look at the floor. I have enough problems. No jealous girl drama for this guy.

"Broke my leg and wore a cast for half of third grade."

The whole class laughs again except for Kayla, me, and Miss Brandel, who must have felt she needed to redirect the class's attention back to our lesson.

"There you go, Billy. You both know football and Jeff knows about injuries. You could work on a story about the appropriate treatment of sports injuries."

"Yeah, you could even wear capes for inspiration," Claire offers a final teasing comment.

"Thank you, Claire! I think we can move on." Miss Brandel's tone has a bit of desperation in it.

The class might have managed to go on without further interruption and laughter if Billy hadn't piped up. "I'm not wearing no cape. It ain't manly."

His buddy Jeff jumps in, "You ever really look at our football pants?"

Even Kayla busts up as Billy begins to sputter.

"Okay, okay everyone, your ticket out of this room is a completed form written neatly enough I won't need to squint." Miss Brandel smiles. "I'm too young for wrinkles and on a teacher's salary, I can't afford Botox. Everyone, settle down. You've got twenty minutes." She hands out forms to students at the first table.

"She's cool," Kayla says, digging through her bag for a pen with the hand I wasn't holding onto behind our work-station.

"Yeah. She'll make us work, but she's funny."

My girlfriend and I smile at each other. Then we stare at each other and smile more. Finally Kayla turns red and breaks up our mutual stare-a-thon by tugging up the top of her blue tank top to better cover her chest. I didn't think I had been looking down there, but I can feel the heat of my face turning red too. I try looking even lower only to notice how long her long legs are as they come out of her white shorts and end with her pretty feet in a pair of flip flops. Then it's flushed face city for me when I recall how my grandma still calls those shoes *thongs*. The thought of that word in a different context is not something I feel comfortable contemplating in front of my girlfriend. Well, not yet.

The fact that I even notice what Kayla is wearing shows me my feelings for her are changing. I now notice things like how her high ponytail accents her facial structure or that her hair ribbons emphasize her eye color. Yup, I am in serious like with some plain old *lustful teen* thrown in.

"What are you putting down for clubs and organiza-tions?"

"I don't know. I'm not much of joiner."

Kayla's polite enough not to acknowledge some of this is because we can't afford to do much extracurricular. After my dad died, Mom used most of the insurance money to pay off the business expenses from his garage. We didn't starve, but there never had been much left over for extras like soccer or Boy Scouts when we were younger.

"I could put down the whole peer group thing. I haven't actually started, but I'm only doing it and dance team." Kayla chews on her pen cap.

"At least now we will be able to add newspaper staff when we start filling out college applications." I shift in my chair. "I'm having more trouble with hobbies. How many stories can I write about playing on an old game system, eating a lot and tossing a rubber ball to a mongrel dog the size of a small skyscraper?"

Kayla giggles. "You could do something on pet owner-ship, but I think Thor is a dog worthy of his own column, not a mere article."

"No doubt. He's certainly a character. Max should be the one to write about him. He loves that dog much more than I do."

Kayla looks thoughtful before suggesting, "You could milk the twin angle. That is something that makes you unique."

"Isn't that an oxymoron?" I retort playfully. "The whole point about being an identical twin is I'm not unique. There's a look alike spare. Max"

"I don't think you and Max look alike at all. You're the cute one." Kayla blushes again.

I look at Kayla's pink face and debate whether I can kiss her without the rest of the class noticing.

A discreet cough indicates Miss Brandel's arrival at our table.

"How are you two doing with your surveys? Stuck on anything?"

Other than each other? Nope. Better clean that answer up for the teacher.

"No. We're getting them filled out."

Kayla nods in agreement.

"Good. For the last question on the survey, try to brainstorm topics of a higher journalistic value than sports scores or public opinion pieces. You'll be writing those articles too, but I would like to see someone come up with a spectacular piece. Think about your life experiences or maybe something from your family histories that could be helpful to the student body. Okay?" She looks for our agreement before sailing off to the next group.

Kayla frowns. "I don't have many experiences with my family that I want to share with the world. Let's see, sister dying, father deserting us, or mother who tries to drink herself into oblivion?" She adds softly, "I don't think so."

I nod to show my understanding. Neither of our kind of family life experiences are the type we want people to read about. Or that we want to write about. We both sit quietly filling out the rest of the form.

What would I write about for our family's most memorable experience? Dad's suicide. What type of writing best fits that?

I could start with a descriptive piece on my father. That would be easy. Physically, Michael Jamison had been a bigger, older version of Max and me. He liked fixing cars and taking photos. People who knew him said he was the first to help out if someone needed it.

G. A. Edwards

To Max and me, he was the guy who would get us milkshakes and talk Mom into letting us have them before supper. Our hero, the guy who never gave us any reason to doubt his love. Until he got depressed and killed himself.

Wonder how much readers would enjoy a step by step process of what led up to his suicide? First, have your best friend and business partner take all of your automotive garage's money to run off with an Indian casino cashier. Next, become so down, you sit in your robe for weeks in a darkened bedroom refusing to interact with everyone who loves you or take the medication the doctors prescribed that could help you. Then, one day suddenly appear for breakfast and act normal for a couple of weeks to make everyone think you're getting better. Finally, a few nights later tell your kids a bedtime story, kiss your wife goodnight, and sneak out sometime before dawn to hang yourself from the rafters of your own bankrupt garage.

And if those writing types aren't appealing, I can go with a simple comparison/contrast of what our lives were like before and after his death? I bet nobody would publish this article after they read my word choices to explain the grief, anger, and confusion we all still feel.

Dad's the one who should have written something. How about a short note informing us what makes a man choose to leave his wife and children? Or an explanation of what we could have done differently to make him want to live? Or maybe just an apology for changing our family forever.

The first couple of times I helped one of my girls, I had to go ahead of time and check out the sites. It's got to be close, private, and with water deep enough to get the job done.

Now, the satellite maps are so helpful. If I want to find a potential body of water, I just enter my address and zoom in on the aerial view. I don't even have to access this information from my own computer. I can use one from anywhere in town. It's how I determined the creek with the clearest and shortest path to the river.

Isn't technology a wonderful thing?

The Killer

6

The nutty aroma of peanut butter hits my nose when I rush through the back door.

"Don't eat everything!" I call into the kitchen to Max while pausing on the entry porch to hang up my backpack and take off my tennis shoes.

"You better hurry," Max jokes.

Our family lives in a small craftsman-style house in the older part of town. I know this, because Mom's obsessed with those DIY television shows. We used to live on the other side of town in a better neighborhood, but Mom had to sell the old house to help satisfy Dad's creditors. She found this one and hired Susan, Kayla's aunt, to come in with her construction guys to renovate this house. It's small enough that Max and I have to share a bedroom, but the back yard had enough room for Thor's doghouse and pen.

Max and Thor are in my favorite room of the house, the kitchen. Max sits at the kitchen island, surrounded by the economy-size jars of peanut butter and jelly, loaf of bread, and two tall glasses of milk. Our normal after-school food fest, Max chomps away at the first of the many sandwiches we will both consume. Thor laps up a bowl of fresh water at his feet while he keeps a keen eye above for falling crumbs.

Without a word, I jump on my stool, slap together a super thick-jelly heavy-sandwich and take a huge bite.

Max finishes most of his sandwich, throws the crusts down to Thor, and takes a huge gulp of milk before making his next sandwich. We both eat voraciously and silently until he asks, "You get the money?"

I nod an affirmative, my mouth is too full to answer. But I reach in my pocket and hand over his cut for the lawn work we did for our next-door neighbors, the Applewhites. They are pretty old and we would mow their lawn for free, but Mr. Applewhite is a feisty WWII Veteran who insists on paying his way. Mrs. Applewhite just likes us to come over and visit. We like to visit too. She bakes a lot of cookies, pies, and cakes.

"You want some more milk?" Max pours his own glass and indicates my half full glass, which I immediately drain and push toward him.

It's good of Max to have everything already out on the table. I do like peanut butter and jelly sandwiches, but they're also the only snack Mom says she can afford for us to eat as much as we want. She's lucky that Max and I usually like the same foods. The truth is, Max and I do have similar interests in most everything. Television shows, video games, and movies are the same things that most of our friends like too.

We're like most siblings, twins or not. At times it's nice to have someone around that has your back and sometimes having a brother and being one is a pain. Like now, as I try to grab for the last two pieces of bread, only to have Max get to them first.

Max laughs and holds the bread over his head. I grope half-heartedly to reach them as Mom walks in the kitchen from the back porch.

"Okay you two, knock it off. Give me a few minutes to rest before I need to change into my referee's outfit. Share, Maxwell James!" Mom orders good-naturedly and absently bends to pet Thor.

Max grins superiorly as he debates and then tosses the heel of the loaf. I catch it with the flashy expertise of an overpaid wide receiver. I opt out of a run to the other side of the house and a touchdown dance in favor of slathering my piece of bread with grape jelly.

"Hi Mom." Max crosses the kitchen to hug her.

Not to be outshone as a good son, I grab a spoon from the dish drainer by the sink, return to the jar to load it up with peanut butter, and hand it to her.

"My heroes." Mom ruffles my hair and then leans her elbows on the island.

We all eat for a few seconds before I open my mouth and say a grape sandwich enhanced, "*Helwhoa smuddr.*"

"Martin Joseph Jamison! Close your mouth," she says before taking another bite of peanut butter and opening her mouth to add, "*Shobbin yur fud to udrz is grussb.*"

That's my mom for you. Mary Jo Reynolds Jamison to others, this is a woman who scolds us, loves us, and makes us laugh while she is doing it. Money issues, Max's medical problems, and the overwhelming responsibilities of maintaining a single parent household could make Mom a bitter person, but she isn't. She chooses to live her life full of smiles and laughter. Max and I are lucky to have her, although we have too much teenage cool to openly admit how much.

Max finishes off his half of sandwich while Mom licks the rest of her peanut butter off the spoon. Thor snuffs a little to show his interest in any extras.

"Sorry Thor. Nothing here for you." Mom shakes her head at our dog.

Thor promptly turns his soulful eyes toward me. I toss the rest of my sandwich toward his awaiting mouth. Maybe grape jelly and bread don't fit the recommended daily guidelines for pet food, but none of us are good at denying our dog anything. We adopted him just after Dad's death on the recommendation of our family's grief counselor. And while nothing or nobody can truly make up for our missing father, Thor manages to be a big comfort to us all. Most especially Max. He and Thor spend many of their evenings going on walks or playing catch in our bungalow's tiny back yard. Thor even sleeps with Max when they can sneak him past Mom.

Mom turns from the sink and fills a glass with water. After a quick drink, she holds the cool glass to her forehead and leans back against the countertop.

"That was good. I wish I had the metabolism of you two to eat all that bread." She sets her glass down. "So, how was school? Anybody got homework?"

Max nods toward me to go first.

"School was good. I've got to finish my math and I need to work on some ideas for newspaper articles."

"That's interesting. What have you come up with?" Mom asks.

"Not much." I reply glumly, remembering my earlier inner rant about articles about Dad, "At least nothing I want to write about."

"I'm sure you'll come up with something." Mom turns to my brother. "What about you, Max? Homework?"

"No. Got it done in class. Regular classes don't have as much as Smarty Marty's advanced ones."

This is true, but it's hard to tell from Max's tone if he resents knowing his classes are easier.

Mom studies him carefully before saying, "Why don't you enjoy some TV until dinner. I need to study some limbs."

Mom's studying to become a physical therapist. She says the job will pay better and she'll work regular office hours. No more rotations of the long hours in her current low-level nursing position.

"Actually, I thought I would take Thor and we would go hang out at Jacob's. It's so quiet over there, it's like somebody di..." Max stops abruptly.

Awkward, since someone *did* die from Jacob's house. Natalee.

We all sit in silence until Mom says, "That'll be fine, Max. I'm sure both you and Thor will be a comfort to him." Mom stands up. "I'm going to grab a shower and do some studying before I start supper. Marty, let me know if you need any help on your work." She smiles. "I can at least try to help you."

"Sure, Mom."

Thor pads over to Max as she leaves the room.

"So Jacob is still having a hard time?" I ask while searching through my bag for my pencil, textbook, and assignment.

"Yeah. Whole family is."

"I don't blame them."

"Me either." Max takes a shuddering breath, "I think Jacob is feeling extra guilty. Me too. We're the ones who showed Natalee the shortcut to the lake's swimming area."

"That sucks. For both of you."

"Don't it ever." Max motions toward the door. "Later, bro. Come on, Thor."

Thor takes one more look to determine if the food is really gone, then follows Max out. Our dog might be named after a Norse god, but it'll take more than doggy super powers to make anyone in Natalee's family feel much better.

"Madison County 911 Dispatch. What is the nature of your emergency?"

"Mi hija Lola is gone. Her padre no return her from visita. Por favor, help!

"Ma'am, please slow down. Who's gone? Who has her?"

"Mi bebe'! Mi Lola! Her padre. He's bad. Bad man."

"Can you give me your name and where you are now? Get Manuel in here. I think this lady's daughter is missing and I need some help to understand her.

911 Dispatch Operator

Music blares from the earphones of my used music player. It's late and I'm tired from a day of school and an evening of wiping out aliens with Max on our game system.

Something like a small pillow or a dirty sock smacks my leg. Taking off my earphones and rolling over in the dark toward Max's side of the room, I say, "You better hope that whatever that was has not been in close proximity with one of your stinky body parts."

"All of my clothes are close to stinky body parts. I'm a teenager. We're gross."

This is why I call him Mr. Literal. Always wants to explain too much and state the obvious. Crap. I just did the same thing.

Max turns toward me even though I can't see him. "Were you asleep?"

"Almost." I sigh, turn off the player and put it on the crate serving as my nightstand. "I was listening to music."

"I thought so."

"Did you want something, Max?" I yawn.

"I can't sleep."

"You'll wish you had in the morning."

His turn to sigh. "Yeah, I know."

It's an unfortunate fact that Max's meds work great to keep him asleep in the morning, but they can take too long each night to help him get to sleep.

"I was just laying here thinking about that girl."

"What girl? The new one with the red hair? Had on the really short purple dress?"

"Not that girl. I saw her too. Ray said that she was fine."

"He probably said she was fine and on her way to being mine."

"You got that right, Marty," Max says this with enthusiasm, but his next statement is subdued. "I meant I was thinking about Natalee."

"Why?" I ask in the darkness.

"I don't know. I feel bad. Jacob wasn't doing too great when I went over there."

"I'll bet." I sit up on the side of my bed.

"Jacob is really down."

"It'll take time. His folks still fighting?"

"No." Max shifts restlessly. "Jacob told me his parents were fighting a lot before and now they aren't talking to each other at all."

"That's bad. But you know it'll take time for everyone to get better. Like it did with us, after Dad died."

There's a moment of silence.

"Are we better, Marty?" Max asks softly, "Really better? Can we ever be?" The creak of his bed tells me he turns on his back. I figure he's staring up at the ceiling and probably trying not to cry.

I don't answer. No good answer to his question. Even all of these years later, my brother thinks about our dad's suicide too much while I try to pretend I never had a father. Leave it to Max to lay our problems out there in the dark. Most of the time I laugh when Max goes into his Mr. Literal kick. This isn't one of the funny times.

I follow his example and turn to stretch out on my back.

A few minutes pass.

Max asks, "Marty, could we do the story?"

"Aw, Max. We're too old."

I don't want to do the story. It's the one thing both of us do that makes us seem crazy. The kind of crazy, the other kids already think Max is and maybe our dad really was at the end.

In the last couple of weeks before Dad died, each night he would come to our room to say goodnight. It had been a long time since he felt up to it. I remember how excited we were when he would whisper his special story to us. It was something he made up and at the time we were too little to realize it was our dad's way of imparting his metaphor for life. Ironic, since Dad must have already been plotting to end his own. It still hurts to think that Max and I were more loose ends for him to tie up before tying that rope up to the rafter.

The actual story isn't the problem. The problem is that after Dad died, Max and I would say the story together every night to comfort us. Every night. Exactly the same way. It's more than just a habit. It's called *echolalia*, or a repetition of sounds and words. It isn't dangerous or even that unusual. It's a method of self-soothing and in a toddler it's perfectly normal. It's not even that unusual for twins to do it together with set roles or parts like we did.

Max interrupts my thoughts, "Please, Marty. I can't get to sleep."

"Did you take your pill?" I ask.

"Yes. And it isn't working fast enough," Max complains.

"Max, you know it upsets Mom when she hears us."

This gets no response from Max's side of the room. What can he say? Once I overheard Mom tell Susan how it freaked her out to hear our childish voices repeating the lines over and over. She must have been relieved to learn medical professionals agree it was probably a temporary condition and that we would outgrow the need to say it. In my case, this proved to be true.

Not so much in Max's. Whether it's that he has more of a natural tendency toward the condition, or whether he simply isn't as far along in accepting Dad's death, he still needs to do the story on the nights he feels stressed. Worry about his best friend and thinking about a little dead girl aren't unexpected emotional triggers, so I'm not surprised he asked. I just don't want or need a reminder of the man who taught it to us or a time in my life I would rather forget.

"Marty, please," Max entreats from his side of the room, "I really can't sleep."

I give in.

"Okay, but keep it down. We don't need Mom to hear us."

"Me either. I *am* sorry."

"I know, Max. Just start your part."

The Robot Twins

Max: "Once in a galaxy far from our own…" Marty: "A robot realized his life power was fading." Both: So he made two new robots."

Max: "Just alike."

Marty: "Because the first robot knew…"

Both: "Two are better than one!

Max: "Together."

Marty: "They would never feel"

Both: "Alone."

Max: "Then the first robot…"

Marty: "Went far away."

Max: "But the two robots…"

Marty: "Always remember that…

Max: "Two are better than one."

Both: "TOGETHER forever!"

Today's farm report has been brought to you by Wilbur's Feed and Grain, where they take pride in providing good nutrition for all of your livestock needs... What? Okay, I'll do it now.

KMON listeners we need your help. Law enforcement officials have issued a Missing Child Alert for seven-year-old Lola Reyes. Says here she's 50 inches tall and weighs 64 pounds. She's got dark brown hair and eyes with a small scar above her left eyebrow. Possibly traveling south in a white pickup with Jorge Reyes, a thirty-two year old male, also with dark brown hair and eyes, approximately 5'10" with a stocky build. His distinguishing marks include a cross tattoo and a series of dots on his hand. Mr. Reyes has a criminal history and is believed to be armed and dangerous.

Listeners, if you see anyone meeting these descriptions, do not approach them, but contact your local law enforcement agencies and the National Center for Missing and Exploited Children's Hotline at 1-800...

Bucky T. Dodd, KMON Radio Deejay

8

"And that's the ballgame! Madison Mules prevail over the Pleasant Grove Panthers twenty-four to ten. Our Kick-'Em-Where-it-Counts Booster Club thanks everyone for coming out tonight. Please drive safely. Wait a second folks. Just got the news the booster club is selling the rest of the hotdogs three for a dollar. Stop by, support our Mules, and grab hot dogs for the whole family," the announcer gives his final advice as the crowd begins the mass exodus to the parking lot.

Click, click, click. I zoom in on the scoreboard's final results before shooting a few pictures of the exiting crowd. Don't expect these last shots to end up in the sports section of the newspaper, but it's good practice. I really like photography, even though it's something that my dad enjoyed too.

A nice cool September evening like this one is a good night to shoot a football game. My press pass allows me access to the field right in the action. Other than having to dive out of the way a couple of times to escape an out of bounds runner, it's going well and is a great chance to people-watch.

"Get back here! You dagblasted stubborn cousin of Satan."

Now here's picture-worthy action, or maybe a contender for one of those funny video shows. School mascot, Monty the Mule, is on the loose.

"Stop him!"

"Here, muley, muley!"

"Run free!"

"Gosh dagnabit! Stubborn mule!"

Others might not agree, but I think this run away mule is the best part of tonight's game.

I grab my camera to get a great action sequence. A mule gone wild, crowd rushing to and fro and a couple of heroic face first dives into the turf made for entertaining photos. I take a couple of shots and as I am packing up, the flyer Claire left with me falls. I grab it and smooth it out to read. Student Council is sponsoring a self-defense class at the school on personal safety for kids. Claire's heard me say my mom was a nurse, so she asked if I would give one to her to post it at the hospital. Madison just had its first Missing Child Alert and they still hadn't found the little girl. I can't even imagine how her mother must feel. My mom would freak out big time if Max or I went missing.

I need to turn the school's camera back in before I go home tonight, but first, I am hoping for a little conversation and even a quick kiss or two with Kayla. I can see her in sparkling spandex waiting for me at the other end of the field. Max can wait a few minutes.

Kayla stands with some other girls on the team, but her face turns toward me as I approach. She smiles and her outfit isn't the only thing that sparkles. Suddenly I can't breathe. My girl's that wonderful.

"Still using the school's camera to become a stalker, I see," she says as I grab her hand. We continue to the exit gates together.

"I see myself more as a spy than a criminal."

"So do government spies, but they do illegal things all of the time." She tosses her ponytail.

"Maybe, but a government blessing goes a long way. And how many government spies do you know anyway?" I ask.

She giggles and her lit-up face, spandex-clad body and sparkly hair bow become too dazzling for me. I try to breathe and think of something intelligent to say.

Finally I give up on *intelligent* and squeeze out the mundane, "Good game, huh?"

"Like you really care that much. I know how you feel about sports," she retorts.

"I gotta admit it was more exciting than I expected. Cool, that Billy got to go in when our quarterback got hurt at the end." I turn red. "The Billy part, I mean. Not that the quarterback got hurt."

Kayla nudges me with her elbow. "I knew what you meant. But it was nice to get a win."

We catch up with the crush of spectators.

"I really like you," I say in a rush.

"What?" Kayla stops in the flow of people, her eyes searching my face.

I can't believe I blurted it out, just like that. Right here. Right now. And right in the middle of everyone. So far Kayla and I haven't voiced our feelings for each other out loud, and I just announce that I like her. I want to repeat it, but the closeness of the crowd and a case of chicken-out syndrome rules my actions instead.

"What did you say?" she asks again.

I look at her and choke. "Uh, I said I like you in your dance. Very synchronized." Not smooth on my part at all.

Kayla studies my face for another second before saying, "That isn't what I thought you said. Thanks."

I like to believe that in another moment I'll man up in spite of the crowd and tell Kayla the truth, but Max and Ray arrive.

"Well, well, if it isn't Madison High's very own dance team star, Kayla Gallagher? How's it shakin'? I would say *f-i-n-e* based on all that movement I saw earlier tonight."

"Shut up, Ray. You say every girl is fine," I say as Kayla and I turn toward them.

"And how is that a bad thing?" Ray grins as evilly as his baby face can.

"Hi Kayla. I am ready to go, Marty," Max assures me.

"In a minute, Max. I still gotta find Miss Brandel and turn in the camera before we leave for home." *And make out with Kayla a little.*

"What? No Way!" Ray exclaims. "Nobody's going home yet. Too early. We're young and single and it's our time to live life on the wild side. Winning football scores means babes in a celebratory mood and upperclasswomen too." He sticks out his chest and shakes imaginary pom-

poms while announcing in a falsetto voice, "The Ray Man plans to s-c-o-r-e!" He attempts a high kick, so poorly executed that the crowd walking nearby gives our group a wider berth.

I'm not single in my mind or Kayla's either, so I give her hand a comforting squeeze and him a glare. "Not cool, Ray. I have my girl right here and Max and I need to get home."

"Yeah, we promised our mom," Max adds.

I roll my eyes. That statement is the kind I wish Max a.k.a Mr. Literal would have enough coolness to know not to say. Fortunately, Kayla saves me from Ray's response by asking, "Isn't that Miss Brandel talking to that older guy in the red and gold Mustangs jacket? By the blue car?"

"I'll be right back." I push through the crowds to Miss Brandel and deliver the camera. I come back to Ray sharing his thoughts on probable after parties.

"Everyone's going out to Quarry Road. It's a little cold for swimming in the lake, but supposed to be kegs all over. I've been pumping weights all week, so I'll be prepared for the keg stands. And all these muscles will make it easier to grab onto the hotties. I've got to find a ride before they all leave. See ya later." Ray walks across the parking lot, but his party game plan changes when we see his parents stop him before he reaches his babe destination.

Max, Kayla and I shake our heads with laughter when we hear Ray's whine in the distance, "Aw, come on! I've got plans tonight!"

"I think Ray's party is over for the night," Kayla says.

"I think it was always over," I agree. "How're you getting home tonight? Your mom coming to get you?"

Kayla lives farther away from the school than we do and I'm not comfortable with her walking all of that way alone in the dark.

"She was supposed to, but she didn't answer the phone earlier when I tried calling." Kayla worries her bottom lip with her teeth.

"Maybe she fell asleep. You want to try again?" I ask.

"Not really. I was hoping you could walk me home."

"He is supposed to walk with me. Mom said," Max interjects.

This is one of those moments when having Max as a brother gets on my nerves. Nobody references their parents in public unless necessary. We all try to act as if we are adults in charge of our destinies. Max never understands when to keep his mouth shut and play along. I glare at Max as I try to decide what to do.

"Oh, that's okay," Kayla says.

"No, it's not."

"I'll try calling her again." Kayla digs her cell phone out of her purse.

I debate options. I can call my mom and she'll come get all of us, Kayla included, and take us home. But Mom works a double shift on Fridays and is probably at home on the couch resting her feet and watching sappy old movies by now. Or Max and I can both walk Kayla home. There's a plan that sucks the romantic possibilities out of this nice fall evening. I'm unexpectedly offered a solution to my dilemma by the return of an unhappy Ray.

"My dad sent me back to ask if anybody needs a ride home."

"I thought you were going out to party with old women." Max looks confused.

"Dude, it is older *girls*, not old ladies."

Ray may be the only teenager in existence that still refers to other guys as 'dude'.

He hops back and forth on his feet in frustration before he continues. "My dad is making me go home now, because I've got to get up early and go over to my grandma's to help put up her storm windows."

Good for Ray's dad. My buddy may not be happy about his evening plans, but I recognize a great solution when I hear it.

"Max, why don't you ride with Ray and I will walk Kayla home? Just tell Mom I will be there in a little while. She wouldn't want Kayla to go alone."

Max might have objected, but he can't refute my logic.

Ray sighs, "Come on, Maxman. Let's go. I gotta say you're not who I was hoping to be next to in a backseat tonight."

Max flashes a final doubting look at me and follows Ray to his family's car.

I never thought about the old quarry when I was looking over the maps. I need to check it out sometime, because it sounds promising. Usually deserted except for weekend parties, easy to get there using the service road, and it has a lake with plenty of the most important requirement.

Water.

The Killer

It's mostly quiet as Kayla and I walk through the neighborhoods to the duplex where she lives with her mom on one side and her aunt on the other. Occasionally we hear a dog bark in the distance or noises from cars on nearby streets, but other than a few loud TV volumes at houses we pass, it's a still night. Not many streetlights in the residential areas of a town Madison's size, so the skies are dark and the stars shine clearly. Our hands are clasped and I'm already anticipating great goodnight kisses when we reach the next block.

"I love looking at the stars, don't you? My little sister Krista and I used to beg to go camping in the yard just so we could lie on our sleeping bags and stare up at them." Kayla's voice sounds sweet in the darkness.

"Max and I used to think stars were lightning bugs that got away. We tried to catch as many as we could, so they wouldn't all float to the sky."

I hear the smile in Kayla's voice. "You missed a few."

"Guess so." I release her hand reluctantly. I want to try out putting my arm around her shoulders too, but I'm nervous about her response. Taking a quick breath, I make my move. I think I let out an audible whew when she doesn't jerk away or elbow my ribs.

"Back where I lived before we all moved here permanently, people don't call them lightning bugs. They're fireflies."

"Okay." Having Kayla this close is giving me a little trouble listening and breathing too.

"Yes," Kayla adds quickly, "I did a report on them. They light up to attract a mate."

In the sudden silence that follows I realize Kayla's nervous too. Maybe a kiss will make her feel more at ease. I'm willing to try it, you know, to help her be more comfortable.

I lean in to kiss her when she adds, "And sometimes instead of mating, the female kills the male and eats him."

I pause in mid-approach. That's not a promising thought. Oh, what the heck. I lean forward to enact a smooth move with a kiss to her lips. And miss her mouth completely, landing my lips right on her nose.

It's really dark.

Kayla lets out a quickly silenced giggle.

"Sorry."

"It's okay," she comforts.

Now it's really quiet. Should I try again? Or should I wait until closer to the next street light, so I don't end up making out with her ear or eyeball or something? Maybe some people can get into that, but I'll settle for some regular kisses and a few of the open-mouthed French variety.

Kayla takes the decision away from me by taking both of her hands to cup my face and pull me forward to line my lips up in the right direction. What a great idea! Wish I had thought of it.

But when I feel the warmth of Kayla's soft body come into closer contact with mine and taste the sweet, lip-glossed sticky goodness of her lips, I'm not thinking of much except how to keep kissing. I gotta say, I try my level best to provide multiple kisses including those of the French variety. I would have tried a few other nationalities of kisses too, if I had known of any. Maybe I should check out the Internet.

Kayla and I eventually break apart to acknowledge our mutual need for oxygen.

"Wow."

"Seconded," I add and bark out a laugh. "You aren't going to eat me now like a lightning bug, are you?"

"What?" Kayla questions before she gets it and laughs too. "Of course not. Those fireflies or lightning bugs or whatever must be stupid to eat someone who could make them feel like this." Kayla puts her head down on my shoulder and snuggles up.

I'm grinning proudly and brightly enough to light up the street. My arms circle Kayla at her waist. This is the point where some guys push their luck and try moving their hands down or up. Not me. Not tonight. I'm perfectly content holding Kayla just as we were. Besides, if she moves away I might miss her mouth again going in for a kiss. That's not a chance I'm willing to take. This is the greatest night of my life so far and my euphoria continues right to the front door of the Kayla's duplex when we meet up with her mom.

Cindy, it turns out, is more of good mood killer than an average mother should be.

"I was wondering where you were." Kayla's mom greets us from just outside the door of her side of the duplex.

A mom waiting at the door isn't going to inspire any more kissing with Kayla as far as I'm concerned. I'm not brave enough to try goodnight kisses with a parent watching.

"I tried to call you and to remind you to come get me, but you didn't answer." Kayla's voice is tight as she quickly lets go of my hand and goes up the sidewalk to her mom. I follow, uncertain whether I should say hello to maintain a good impression or leave for home.

"I must have been in the shower," Mrs. Gallagher, who always insists I call her Cindy, explains in a flippant tone. After a moment of nobody saying anything she adds, "Hi, Marty. Thanks for walking Kayla home. She'll say goodnight now."

Kayla's mom usually seems to like me, but she has her purse on her shoulder and it appears she's going out and I'm being sent home.

"Mom, can't Marty come in for a few minutes?" She stares suspiciously at the purse. "Are we going somewhere?"

"No, Kayla, we aren't going anywhere. I'm going out with a couple of old friends, and you know no boys are allowed here if I'm not home. Susan's still at that banquet."

Cindy's vocal inflection indicates the friendly tone of the conversation is deteriorating rapidly. "Goodnight, Marty."

"Marty, don't leave," Kayla calls over her shoulder before hissing to her mother, "Mom, you promised!"

"Kayla Marie Gallagher, I'm the adult. Just because I am going out, it doesn't mean…"

When a mom leads with someone's full name, it means trouble. I want to escape this drama and get out of here. I give up on the idea of more kissing tonight and say goodnight to hurry down the sidewalk. I would have gotten away, but Cindy's ride pulls up.

And what a ride it is. The truck's red and chrome and so high off the ground I can walk underneath it. Huge speakers in the bed of the truck blare out a classic rock anthem. The thumping bass line makes the ground move under my feet. I watch in awe as a huge man jumps out of the passenger door and drains his beer can before pitching it in the truck bed, barely missing the speakers. When Cindy comes up from behind me to join him, they hug and he tosses her up into the cab. He isn't even all the way in the truck when it roars off, but not before I read the tailgate slogan, *Chug Til Ya Can't Feel No Pain*.

I agree with Kayla. These are not the best friends for a recovering alcoholic like Cindy.

I turn back to see Kayla's profile haloed in the porch light. I can see the glint of tears glistening on her cheek and this is the kind of sparkle on her face I don't want to see. When I take a step toward her, softly calling her name, she says calmly, "Go home now, Marty. You can't help me fix her. Nobody can."

She turns and heads in through the unlocked front door, and I hear the distinct click of the lock that signals our evening together is over.

I begin the walk to my house. My plan tonight had been to get Kayla home safe and sound. I have been successful, but I sure wish I could add happy to those adjectives.

I was down to the diner getting some coffee and a piece of pie and I heard they picked up that Reyes guy they talked about on the Missing Child Alert. The one that 'posedly took off with his little girl and tried to make it to Mexico.

Deputy said truck driver down south spotted the fella on I-35 and called in. That Reyes led cops on a chase a'fore they caught 'im over near Salado in Texas. Truck was full of stolen generators, but no sign of the girl.

Guess that guy wouldn't say nothin' at all 'til they brung up his missing kid. Then he 'posedly dropped to the floor screamin' his innocence, crossing hisself, and saying prayers to that Guadalupe lady. Jus' begged them officers to find his la hija, his angel.

Could be somebody else got that girl.
Lowell Cooper-Local Coffee Drinker

10

I enter our house after leaving Kayla's hoping to jump straight into bed. It's been a long day, and tonight has been such a mix of emotional highs and lows that I just want to hide in the darkness.

No such luck.

"Marty, did you get Kayla home okay?" Mom calls softly from the living room as I try to hurry down the hall.

I hesitate.

"Marty?"

Giving up, I head into the living room. Mom's in her sweats lying on one end of the couch with Thor sprawling across her feet like a smelly fur comforter. One of those novels with a hot chick and muscular guy on the front rests spine side up on the coffee table. Mom calls these books her mind candy and says they are full of damsels in distress, handsome heroes, and happy endings. Maybe I should read one for pointers. I'm not feeling like much of hero after leaving my own damsel so distressed.

I sit down and Thor quits snoring long enough to look me over before settling back down. Mom hands me her bowl of potato chips. Being the mother of teen boys has taught her food is always welcome.

"Hey, Mom." I say before taking a crunchy mouthful.

"Hey, son. How did the photography go?"

I swallow my chips first. Mom's liable to smack me with a throw pillow if I talk with my mouth full.

"Pretty good. I got a couple of decent shots. The runaway mule was great. I might make this week's paper front page with those shots. Oh, and we won the game."

"Yes, Max told me about when the O'Rears dropped him off. He said you walked Kayla home."

"Yeah." I say shortly, trying to evade the next question I know she'll ask.

"Was there a problem that Cindy couldn't come and get Kayla?"

Mom gets along with Cindy and tries not to judge her for her drinking problem. Mom always says that a death in the family is difficult for everyone and losing a child would be the worst. But Mom's first allegiance in any situation is to make certain that the living children are being taken care of appropriately.

"Marty?"

I take another handful of chips to delay telling her Kayla's mom had been so concerned with going out to drink that she forgot to pick Kayla up. Again. Mom will tell Kayla's aunt Susan. They tell each other everything. I don't know if Kayla wants her aunt to know.

It's a lost cause, because one don't-you-lie-to-your-mother look from her and I'll confess whatever she wants to know. So far tonight, she hasn't given me the look, but it might pop out of her parenting arsenal at any moment. I go ahead and spill the beans before she does it.

"Yeah, there was a problem. When Kayla and I got to the house, her mom was on her way out the door with friends."

"Was she drunk?"

That's my mom for you. She's direct when it comes to asking the tough questions. I don't think she was always this way, but Dad's suicide left a lot of unanswered questions for everybody. Now she won't take any chances. She asks.

"I don't think so. She seemed okay when she left."

"How did Kayla take it?"

"Bad. There was yelling and crying." I set the bowl of chips down on the coffee table. I'm not so hungry anymore.

"What did Susan say when this happened? Didn't she notice?" Mom's looking right at me now.

"She wasn't home yet from some banquet."

"Oh that's right. I forgot that was tonight." Mom fiddles with the drawstring of her sweatpants for a moment before asking, "Kayla's home alone?"

I nod again, not trusting myself to speak. I'm the jerk who left her there.

"I think one of us should call and check on her. Do you want to do it?" Mom gets up, dislodging Thor to dig through her purse for her cell phone.

"No, you. I don't know what to say to her."

I like Kayla and I don't want to say anything to blow our relationship up when we're just getting to the good stuff. That's what I tell myself in my brain, but I really just don't want to hear her crying on the phone.

Mom calls and waits, but nobody answers. She hangs up without leaving a message.

"I'll try Susan."

"Do you have to? She'll get upset. Kayla hates it when Susan and Cindy argue." I punch at one of the couch's throw pillows in agitation.

"Yes, yes, I think I should. Susan will be upset if she finds out that we know about this and don't tell her. And Kayla shouldn't be alone if she is upset."

Dang, I swear that woman knows just what to say to make me feel guilty without even trying. She looks at me curiously before pushing Susan's quick number. I reach over and grab more chips to munch on nervously while Mom explains to Susan what happened.

When the call ends, Mom puts the phone on the coffee table and reaches for the remote.

"Susan's almost home. She'll check on Kayla and give us a call back. You want to watch some TV while we wait? You can pick."

For once, chilling out in front of the TV doesn't sound too appealing, but it beats just worrying. We spend the next few minutes staring at a cheesy old sci-fi movie. Then the phone buzzes. Thor sits up and leans on my leg for some petting.

"Hello, Susan."

My attention is on this conversation and not on the TV battle of man-eating monsters filmed with extremely poor visual effects.

"Okay, you went over and checked. And Kayla was all covered up asleep in her bed. That's good." It's nice of my mom to repeat the details for me.

And now that I know Kayla isn't up worrying about her own mom, I am ready to sleep too. Especially when I hear the topic of Mom's next comment.

"This lawyer that you met there, is he handsome?"

I give Thor a final pat before standing up and stretching. I bend down and pick up the empty chip bowl to drop off in the kitchen on my way to the bedroom.

I figure it's the polite thing to do since I ate all of Mom's chips. Again.

Fair week means there's a lot going on and more people than normal in Madison. I want to relax like everybody else, but things happen. Sometimes to the girls and in my life, too. That's why I have to be ready to go at all times.

Where there's a will, there's a way, people always say.

The Killer

"Are you finished with your plate, Marty? It looks like it's about to give up and collapse." Kayla's mom gestures toward my now soggy paper plate. Only a short time ago, its sections held two grilled burgers, a hot dog, a mondo helping of homemade potato salad and spicy baked beans.

I'm enjoying the spoils of a bar-be-que before the Madison Fall Festival kicks off with its annual parade. Missouri even surprised everyone with October weather in the seventies, allowing us to eat outside in our shirtsleeves on the duplex's shared back deck.

"Sure." I hand her my plate, but keep my fork to lick clean in preparation for my next course, Susan's homemade chocolate sheet cake. Does anyone else hear the angel choir too? Before I could make my move into this food version of heaven on earth, Mom ruins my plan.

"Marty, I've got to run your brother over to the house to pick up the shirt the activity center wants him to wear. Can you take all of the lawn chairs to the front yard while I am gone?"

Leave it to Max to get out of lawn chair duty. Our school found him a job at the local activity center. He mostly checks out balls and other equipment, but he sweeps the gym floor in between games too. This afternoon the center has him walking in the town parade to pass out flyers and candy along the route to encourage families to let kids come in. Kayla still goes there once a week to do the peer mentoring and would have been doing the same thing, but she's marching with the dance team.

I sigh dramatically. "I guess. So much for my dessert plans."

"Where would you put it?" Kayla giggles as she eyes my protruding belly.

"Don't be a doubter!"

"Really, a *doubter*? What college prep list did you get that one from?" Kayla challenges.

"It's like a hater only they're more undecided." I throw my arm around her and give a quick squeeze.

"The cake can wait until after the parade," Mom says.

"You better not be eating all of the cake while I am marching by in the parade," Max warns, "I might *accidentally* knock you unconscious with a handful of hard candy we throw out."

Susan, Cindy, Mom, Kayla and I laugh at his seriousness.

"Kayla, if you want to go ahead and get your dance team outfit on, Max and I can give you a ride to the parade starting point," Mom offers.

"That would be great." Kayla looks at me, "Be right back."

"Even though I am so full I could take a nap, the rest of this food won't put itself away." Susan rises to clear the table.

I surrender my dirty fork for washing and start grabbing and folding chairs, because it looks like there will be no cake until after the parade. Cindy stands up from where she had been scraping plates and joins Susan in clearing. Mom and Max follow the sidewalk around duplexes to the driveway. I snitch the last hot dog resting on the platter, polish it off, and head around to the front with the chairs.

Other people up and down the street are also lining up their own chairs and laying out blankets for prime parade viewing spots. I get the chairs set and walk over to grab my camera bag from the car before Mom drives off with it.

Once Mom realized I was taking pictures for my newspaper class she gave me all of Dad's old camera equipment. He had been a pretty good amateur photographer. The equipment isn't the latest model, but it all works. I play around every week or so practicing some of the techniques we're learning about in class.

Kayla runs out of the duplex, blowing me a kiss before jumping in the car with Mom and Max. I grin at her. I grin even more when the car drives by. Using his fingers in the universal "V" shape and gesturing between his eyes and my mouth, Max indicates he'll be watching to see if I'm eating the cake. I respond with an exaggerated chomping motion.

Susan sticks her head out the door. "Marty, would you like more iced tea or a pop?"

"I'm good for now. Thank you."

I sit down in one the chairs to check the settings on the camera. I'm not required to take photos of the parade, but I want to record the event. The Madison Fair Festival is one of my family's favorite activities. It's always the first week of October, lasts for three days, and the weather isn't usually too bad. Carnival rides set up downtown, contests are held for everything from the biggest vegetables to youngest baby to ugliest dog. A fairgoer can buy greasy, delicious food, listen to free music of multiple genres, knock teachers and police officers into the dunking tank, and enter drawings for homemade quilts or even your own horse.

More importantly to each of the members of our family, the fair comes directly after the anniversary of Dad's suicide on October first. Mom, Max, and me, all try to ignore the significance of that date, but even after all of these years we still fail miserably. Max is more depressed than normal. I am irritable. Even Mom, who manages to be perky throughout the other fifty-one weeks of the year, is down and only gets happy again because she knows the fair is coming to town to distract us from our mutual sorrow.

Cindy, Kayla's mom, suddenly says from behind me, "I went ahead and brought you a bottle of water in case you get thirsty."

"Thanks."

Cindy sits in the chair next to me. Neither one of us say anything for a few minutes as we watch cars racing up and down the street. Although we have known each other for years, my interactions alone with Cindy have been few. She's spent so much time in rehab. Now she's my girlfriend's mother. It's weird. I haven't even seen Cindy since the night she sent me home after the football game. I knew from Kayla that her mom hadn't come home until the next morning and she wasn't sober. When she sobered up, she immediately called her AA sponsor for help. I'm pretty sure things are going better, because Kayla and Susan haven't seemed upset much.

I take a quick look at Cindy to find her staring at the glass of tea in her hand.

"Marty, I want to tell you I am sorry," she says, "for acting that way the night you walked Kayla home. I appreciated that you got her home safely."

"That's okay. I was happy to be with Kayla," I try to reassure her. It really isn't okay that she had left Kayla without a ride and upset her by going out and getting drunk, but Cindy looks pretty broken up about what she did.

We sit in silence some more and I fiddle with the camera to cover being uncomfortable.

"Your mom says you're good with the camera. Like your dad was."

I grit my teeth at her comparison to my father, but get out, "Thank you."

"You know Kayla's dad Will wouldn't have anything to do with her before he died." Cindy traces a bead of condensation down the side of her glass with her finger.

"Yeah, she told me." I don't think I can be more confused about the direction of this conversation.

Cindy suddenly looks up. "I'm going to be blunt with you. Kayla is the one good thing I have ever done in my life. I won't bother making excuses for my problem with alcohol, but I don't know if you realize how much losing Krista changed our lives. Especially for Kayla. First she lost Krista, then her dad and for a while, me too."

This emotional stuff is beyond me, so I sit without comment waiting to see what she says next.

"I'm sorry. You're a nice boy. I just need you to realize…Kayla isn't just a *part* of my life. She is my life. I don't want anyone to ever hurt her again."

"I don't want her hurt either," I protest.

"I can tell that about you. But please don't act like you care about her and then let her down. I don't think she can handle someone else in her life doing it to her again." She takes a drink from her glass of tea while the ice clinks from the tremors of her hand.

I set the camera down in the bag with care. My own hands are shaking with anger now. She's the one disappointing Kayla, not me. I don't need a lecture on being responsible from someone who can't stay sober enough to have custody of her own kid.

I look Cindy directly in the eyes. "My *father* taught me all about how much it hurts when someone lets you down. What's left of my family works hard not to let others down. It's why my mom puts in so many hours at the hospital helping others. It's why Max is such a good friend that he goes over to his buddy's house even though Jacob stays shut up in his room refusing to talk to him. It's why I'll always do my best to never let Kayla down or anybody else."

Cindy's brows furrow as she appears to measure the sincerity of my statements. "I'm sorry for upsetting you. It's obvious you understand why this topic is important." She takes a deep drink of her tea and adds, "I'm glad Kayla can count on you, Marty."

I nod. I feel a little better to realize her mom cares enough about Kayla to question me. While Cindy might love drinking alcohol, she seems to love her daughter more. Too bad Cindy's actions later that night will cause me to question this.

Unfortunately, Kayla will be forced to wonder too.

Melissa Joe Cotton, hold on to Mommy's hand now. I said hold on.

That's it. Your time at the fair is over tonight, Sassy Missy. No more rides or games for little girls who don't listen. You'll be lucky if I don't take you to the car and give you a little old-fashioned attitude adjustment. And when we get home you can just march your little self right in and get in your bed.

Mommy's going to bed too. She has to be at work first thing in the morning anyway.

Peggy Cotton-Mother

12

I stand with other fair goers near the grandstand on Main Street. Kayla's busy waiting to see if any of the little girls she works with at the activity center will win the junior queen contest. Then we'll hit the midway together to ride some rides. I want to win Kayla a stuffed animal or something in one of the games of chance. I'm thinking about us making out at the top of the Ferris wheel and don't notice Max, Ray, and Billy until they cover me in a sneak attack of foam spray string. I don't have to wonder what they got as their prizes on the midway.

"Jerks!" I state emphatically while laughing and trying to dig my way out of the string now all over my hoodie and dark hair.

Ray bows formally and deeply, "At your service, sir." He is a guy who attends a few too many Renaissance Fairs, in my opinion.

"We got you good, Marty," Billy is nearly shouting. He gets a little excited during the fair and his volume control is nonexistent.

"Sorry about that, big brother," says Max. His grin makes his remorse doubtful, but he does bend over to help me pick up the debris and walks it over to the nearby trashcan.

"We been lookin' for you. We want you to come ride the Thunder Roller with us," Billy yells.

Max adds, "It's got two upside down loops this year."

The loud applause signals the announcement of the new little queen's name nearly blocks out my, "Cool." I look at the big plush toy dog in Ray's arms. "Nice dog, Ray. Couldn't get a date?"

"I won him at the baseball game. You know I am a pitching phenomenon." Ray brags with reason. He really is. "I named my not-so-little stuffed friend 'Zeus'. He's my ticket to the sweet ladies. No girl can resist the combination of puppy love and the Rayman."

We groan, but know he's correct about the stuffed animal part anyway. Girls love it when guys win them something on the midway. And guys? We try to act real tough to establish our imaginary *street cred*, but we really are little boys when it comes to carnival rides and games. The faster the rides and the bigger the prizes, the better. I might have gone to the midway with the guys too, but Ray whistles his trademark *hot-babes-a'walking* signal and we all turn to see where he's looking. I mean, carnival rides are great, but puberty has a strong enough grip on all of us to know chicks rule. I puff up with pride to see one of the three girls he's admiring is mine. Then again, I might have to punch him for it. I'm more than satisfied when Kayla comes to stand next to me and grabs my hand.

Ray moves immediately with doggy in arm to slide in between a couple of the girls on the dance team with Kayla. "Hello, Lady Jenna and Lady Alyssa. Let me introduce you to my little friend, Zeus. He's got all of the qualities of a god, just like me."

Everyone laughs except for Ray when the girls roll their eyes and stick their elbows into his sides.

Kayla reaches up and pulls out a piece of the foam string caught in my hair. "You threw away all of your pretty decorations. I thought you looked a like a human party favor," she teases.

"If that was a party, then I am a party pooper. It's a good thing I got my hair cut this week, or I'd still be buried under the party." I drop her hand to put my arm around her waist. I might not be brave enough to show my affection overtly in front of our families, but it's nighttime now with no moms in sight.

Billy emphasizes his agreement by bobbing his head up and down, "I liked it. You looked like that neon thing from the swamp on the old cartoons."

"That's a good one." Ray adds. "I was thinking more Medusa. I did a report on her for Mythology last year. Did ya know she used to be hot before the whole snake thing?" Ray's shoulder companions elbow him in the sides again. "Ouch! Seriously, do a search on it."

"Can we go ride the rides now? I've got more tickets," Billy yells.

"Dude, do you have to be so loud?" Ray asks.

"Yes, I think I do." Billy says in a serious manner.

We all laugh at him.

Max looks around at the gathered group. "We still have an odd number."

"No problem," Ray says, "Billy here, can ride with my dog. Just don't kiss it when you two ride the Ferris wheel."

"Hey, I ain't gonna kiss no dogs!" Billy croaks.

"Me either," Ray says, planting a quick kiss on Jenna's cheek and then another on Alyssa's.

The girls giggle.

"Come on, Max. You can borrow one of my lovely ladies." Ray shoves his dog into Billy's arms with the instruction to bring his date before leading his ladies onward.

Billy looks down at the dog, huffs, and follows the other three.

Max peers at Kayla and me, asking, "You two coming?"

I squeeze Kayla's waist. "We'll catch up with you. We're gonna walk around a little."

"But we always ride to..." Max shakes his head disbelievingly and stomps off.

Now Kayla and I are alone together. Well, as alone as a couple can be with people passing by on all sides.

"I think Max is mad at us."

"Probably. I usually ride stuff with him during the fair.

"I know. Do you want to go with him?" she asks.

"No, I can ride some with him later. I'm where I want to be right now."

"Me too."

"Let's go."

We take off and our night just gets better from there. We try most of the different rides and kiss at the top of the Ferris wheel with each rotation before we catch up with the others to hang out and play some games. Ray even uses his phenomenal pitching skills to win a big stuffed dog for Kayla after I'm only able to manage a tiny, cheap plastic snake.

I liked that little snake much more than the big one I'm about to meet.

"Cerebus. Ray won it and he say's the name has to be Greek and that's the only dog I can think of from mythology," Kayla states her position on the dog's moniker.

"But this dog doesn't have three heads, and it's a girl. Notice the pink and purple," I tease.

"Where does it say pink and purple are only girl colors? This jacket of yours that I'm wearing looks like a dark purple to me."

"Hey, I already explained my Nana sent that hoodie. I have to like it. As for pink and purple being girl colors, duh, all toymakers and elves know this. And Barbies. Barbies always wear pink and purple. It's in their teeny, tiny contracts."

"Whatever! I decree my dog is and forever will be known as Cerebus." Kayla makes a sweeping arm gesture to emphasize her decree.

"Yes, your majesty." Now I sound like I'm the one who's been to too many Renaissance festivals.

Kayla laughs and hugs her dog closer. I hug Kayla closer too, pretending it's due to the night turning chilly. We're walking back to her place and have left the bright lights of the midway behind. Not too many people are out in this part of town this late, but we just passed the location of the Annual beer garden. The police and neighbors complain every year to the city council trying to get it banned, because of the noise and craziness. But beer drinking and live music are a pretty popular combination with a number of local voters.

Our focus on each other prevents us from noticing the couple up ahead and this makes for an unpleasant surprise. It's Cindy, drunk, and accompanied by a very large man. It looks like he's helping her remain upright through the use of his hands all over her body. Cindy's laughing and doesn't seem upset with his method, but Kayla stops dead and then thrusts her dog in my arms before running toward the couple. She shoves her way in between them.

Smack. "Get off of her!" *Smack. Smack.* "Just leave her alone, you creep!" *Smack!*

Oh crap! Kayla is slapping the chest of the really big guy who now looms over her in the near darkness. Is she crazy? Yes. I think she would punch him in his face, but he's simply too tall.

I hurry across the street, Cerebus in tow, to offer my own fists in case the guy tries to hit Kayla back. If nothing else, the stuffed dog will offer some protection when I get pummeled to death by that titan of a man. Thank goodness Cindy pulls her daughter back and drunkenly tries to hug her. It's the wrong response, but it beats the big guy ripping Kayla's head off.

"Kayla, baby. I thought you was at the…uh, fair." Cindy slurs out. "Dis is my frien' Steve."

Steve isn't the same guy who picked Cindy up at the duplex before. The tattoos on his arm are different. To me, these tats are more like the examples on documentaries about outlaw bikers than the ones of the redneck monster truckers. I don't claim to be an expert in this field.

"The fair's almost over for tonight. And, you told me you would stay home," Kayla chokes out through her clenched teeth.

"Now Kayla, don't be like that. An old frien' came over and asked me out to visit the beer garden."

"Mom, you promised. No drinking!" Kayla roars.

The last time and only time I had been in this situation with Kayla, she'd been upset, but quiet. Tonight she's angry. Really angry. And scary. And loud. Billy's earlier excess volume was a whisper compared to what I now know Kayla is capable of producing. She glares at the big guy like she wants to hit him some more.

Man, I hope she doesn't. Steve is at least six four, probably weighing in around two hundred fifty pounds with a shaved head and those numerous tattoos on his arms, shoulders, and chest. I don't want to judge the man unfairly, but he has the look of a killer. You know, just a jeans, biker boots, and leather vest no-shirt-in-October kind of guy.

"Kayla, don't you talk like that to me! I'm yur mud… der."

"Some mother you are. You're so drunk, you can't even say it."

"Scuse us!" Cindy grabs Kayla by the arm and drags her several feet away where they can trade insults with more privacy. This leaves me alone with Steve, who I'm trying not to look at in the face. All the nature shows say the best way to survive an encounter with a wild animal is to be submissive and not present a challenge by staring directly into their eyes. I close my eyes and hug Cerebus closer, realizing the fair will no longer be a favorite activity of my family if I die tonight.

"Nice dog," Steve says politely, making me jump mightily. "You win it?"

"Yeah." I improvise. "I crushed a car's whole quarter panel in with one hit."

There really is an old car to hit with a sledgehammer if people pay the two-dollar fee. Maybe that isn't impressive enough to a guy of Steve's size and life experience, so I add a blatant lie. "Yeah, I smash lots of things. Use my own customized sledgehammer. I'm kind of famous for it."

"Hmmm." Steve utters. He looks me over and I can see he doubts my claim to fame.

Steve, the Goliath biker and I wait some more until I feel the need to break our silence. "Did it hurt to get all those tattoos, Steve?" I croak and then cringe. What a stupid question. Never ever mention the word *hurt* to someone built like Steve.

"Call me Snake," he invites. "Cindy and my momma are about the only people who still call me Steve. See. It's Snake." He leans near me and I prepare to sacrifice the stuffed dog first. Then I realize he's simply leaning into the light so he can pull back one side of his vest to flex the huge cobra adorning his chest and abdomen. It's documentary-worthy to witness how much he can make that thing writhe back and forth using his immense muscles.

"And yeah, tattoos hurt. Lot worse than those little hits from your girlfriend. Feels a lot like a sledgehammer." He hit one of his fists onto the palm of his other hand to emphasize the point and I can't explain how high I jump. But it's high.

Steve suddenly shows his teeth at me. I think, he's grinning. Could he be trying to joke with me about my sledgehammer comments? Does a guy like Steve…uh, Snake…uh, whatever… make jokes? I take a step further away. What if he's some freak who only tells jokes to make his victims smile right before he knifes them?

Suddenly, Cindy rears back and tries to slap Kayla across the face. She hits her daughter's shoulder instead, because she's drunk. Kayla screeches that we're leaving and takes off down the street. I nod a hesitant goodbye to Snake, who—horrors—extends his hand out to shake. I comply as gingerly as possible. Then I hurry after Kayla, still clutching her big pink and purple stuffed dog tightly in my hands. Both of them.

Know we haven't forgotten that awful day,
When your blessed self went so far away.
Found resting, P.J.'s and ponytail just so,
We're all so sorry you had to go.
Our hearts still feel so much pain.
No day will ever be the same,
Remembering our floating angel, sweet Natalee,
May your beautiful soul rise up and fly free.

Poem mailed to the Petersons

13

"Good morning, son number one," Mom, already dressed for work in pastel scrubs, chirps at me before taking a bite of her toast. She's sitting at the kitchen table, doing her usual morning multi-tasking of eating and studying her notes for her physical therapy classes. Thor sits at her feet, vainly employing his puppy dog look for possible handouts.

"Morning, number one Mom."

We say the same thing every day.

Mom once read an article on parenting twins that stresses how important it is for a parent to spend time alone with each child. Mom embraced the idea ever since Max and I had been little. Max and I will never admit it, but we both like not having to share every minute of our time with Mom. Now that we are older she and Max take Thor for a walk through the neighborhood most nights. Our shared time together occurs in the a.m. while Max sleeps in. Mornings, I look and act a lot like a caveman, but Mom doesn't mind.

Utilizing caveman skills, I hunt up a bowl and spoon and gather some cereal and milk before sitting down across from Mom. Thor positions himself at my feet and turns his hopeful eyes in my direction.

A couple of mouthfuls into my crunching, Mom gives up studying and closes her notebook. "I put some money out for you to go to the fair this afternoon if you want, but your brother is grounded."

Even with all of the Kayla drama, I got home before Max last night and immediately crashed, so I missed the reason for this.

"What'd he do?" I ask. I'm surprised. Max usually doesn't do much to get grounded. Being home on time is the one thing Mom's really picky about. Probably because the night Dad disappeared from the house, she was the one who discovered he had left the house and waited for him to come home. She's also the one who went looking and found him hanging from the rafters at the garage.

"He ran around with friends at the fair and ignored the eleven o'clock curfew and didn't call. It was after one o'clock before he showed up."

"Whoops."

"Whoops, is right. When I asked him where he had been, he tried to tell me he wasn't sure."

"Did he fall asleep somewhere and sleepwalk or something?" I ask this in jest. I figure Billy or Ray talked him into doing something stupid. Max hangs out with them more now that Jacob confines himself to his house most of the time.

"No. I believe he simply chose to stay out and now he will face the consequences."

Mom's lack of sleep from waiting up and having worried about Max shows in the irritation evident in her voice. Mom must realize this, because she changes the subject.

"I saw you and Kayla on some rides together. Did you two have a good time?"

"Yeah. Mostly. "

I take another a bite and grimace as I think of Cindy trying to slap my girlfriend. Last night went like this. Kayla reaches home and she's still in a rage. She disappears in her front door and locks it so quickly, I don't get a hug or a kiss or even a goodbye. I stand under the porch light uncertainly holding Cerebus and wondering if Kayla will let me in if I knock. I'm not going to be the boyfriend who makes the mistake of leaving her alone again. Then through lighted window I see Susan come in the living room and throw her arms around Kayla and I decide it's safe to go home. It isn't the first time they will comfort each other because of Cindy's actions. I leave Cerebus on the porch pulling guard duty in all of his stuffed dog glory.

I put my spoon down to answer the question on Mom's face. "Cindy."

"Again?" Mom sighs.

"Yeah, again." I sigh too. "It was bad. We met her on the street when I was walking Kayla home. They yelled at each other."

"Yesterday, Cindy said she promised to stay away from the fair, so she wouldn't be tempted."

I take another bite to crunchily confess all. Maybe what I'm about to tell Mom is so awful she won't even try to correct my manners.

"Well, Cindy must have changed her plans, because she'd already been to the beer garden and was making out with some scary guy by the time we saw her. Kayla went nuts. She ran up and started smacking the crap out the guy, but he didn't do anything back. Then Cindy and Kayla screamed at each other. Cindy tried to hit her too, but she was too drunk and missed."

"Well, that is just horrible. I don't blame Kayla for being upset." Mom is in full "save the children" mode now. "Who was the man?"

"He said his name was Steve." I swallow before adding wryly and thankfully flexing the fingers of *both* of my hands, "He goes by Snake, if that helps."

"Snake! Oh my…" I'm saved from hearing the ending of her exclamation, when the phone rings and Mom hops up righteously.

"Hello! Oh hi, Jane. No, everything's okay. Just eating breakfast with my son before coming in. What's up?" Mom continues while I fish out the last bite of cereal.

When I tip my bowl up to drink the leftover milk, Mom starts talking in a voice that tells me something is wrong.

"Oh, no! Not another girl. What is going on in this town? How long has she been gone? And nobody has seen her? The police…that's terrible!"

Milk slops over the bowl's rim. Some of it lands on my shirt I wear with shorts for sleeping. A little splashes down on the corner of the table with most of it landing on the floor where Thor takes care of cleanup. I grab up a paper napkin and mop up while Mom listens and leans her body back against the wall. It's something I've seen her do before when she's stressed, so she won't pass out.

"No, it's no trouble. I'll get right down there." Mom hangs up and gets her shoes and sits down in her chair to get them tied.

"Marty, I've got to go. Peggy Cotton, one of our CNA's, got up this morning to come into work and when she checked the kids, little Melissa was missing. Jane said police think somebody took her, because bedroom window screen was cut from the outside. I've got to get in to the hospital to help out until the relief nurse arrives. Two little girls disappearing like this in a town our size makes me wonder what is happening to the world." Mom grabs her purse and rushes for the door. She suddenly stops and retraces her path across the kitchen to kiss me on the cheek before adding, "Be safe."

For once, I didn't object to the kiss or her protectiveness.

Couple of fisherman downriver come 'cross what was left of Lola Reyes in some brush along the bank. 'Course there wasn't much of the poor little thing after the animals had been at her. Had to do DNA tests just to figure out she was a girl and where she'd come from.

First we thought that Reyes fella might've killed his daughter and dumped her in the creek before heading down Mexico way. Man with a record knows his way 'round the legal system.

But then the fair came and the little Cotton girl was gone and everybody's way of thinkin' about that little Lola Reyes' disappearance changed. Decided we needed to take a harder look at the Peterson girl's death.

Town the size of Madison has this many girls missing or dead? Sounds like more than a coincidence to me.

Harold "Chet" Hawkins-Madison Police Chief

14

Max lumbers in with a bowl of cereal and plops down on the other end of the couch. It's just after nine and Thor snores from his resting place on the rug in front of the television stand. My photography bag is in front of me as I organize it while watching some show where a guy reviews new video games. I'm trying to distract myself from calling Kayla's phone again. She's not answering and I'm close to crossing the line to *needy* boyfriend. I keep telling myself I simply want to be sure that she's okay. Maybe she's angry, because I didn't stop her mom from trying to hit her or I didn't stay with her. I hope she doesn't think I was having fun with Snake.

"I got grounded." Max pauses in his cereal chomping to announce.

"I heard."

"It's stupid. The whole night was stupid too. Mom's being stupid too!"

Somebody woke up on the wrong side of the bed.

"Really stupid," Max repeats.

I study my brother. He seems to be living a little dangerously for his usual demeanor and *modus operandi.*

First he gets grounded for staying out late, and now he's breaking Mom's cardinal rule of no milk products consumed in the living room. A rule invoked after an earlier spill that had ended in her favorite chair being dragged out to the curb for the trash truck after it developed the foul stench of soured milk.

"So where were you?"

"Don't worry about it." He sullenly takes a bite of his cereal.

Maybe Max is outgrowing his medication levels again. Every time this happens he becomes surly until his chemical levels get back under control. Then again, his doctor often tells the parents of his patients that it's hard to determine the difference between normal surly teenage-itis or behavior worthy of medication changes.

When Max moves his spoon to his mouth I notice part of his hand is covered in black.

"What happened?"

He glances down but says nothing.

"Max, are you okay? I asked what happened to your hand."

"Just leave me alone, Marty. You don't have time for my problems anymore. You're always too busy with Kayla."

Ouch!

"Max, that's not true."

"Yessssitttisss!" Max mumbles through the chewing. Once he swallows, he adds, "How come you aren't with her now? What'd you do? Act like a jerk again and make her mad?"

Siblings know just where to put the knife. And how to retaliate if cut. I move my camera bag carefully to the side of the couch. I whistle for Thor to wake up. He'll want to be ready to lick up the evidence of my brother's breakfast when I start pounding on Max.

Ring. This could be Kayla. My immediate plan of brother on brother poundage is thwarted as I turn and grab up the receiver of the phone we keep on the end table.

"Hello."

It's not the girl of my dreams. It's the high school counselor. Suddenly, Max and I have something much more important to do than eating, fighting, or even me contacting my girlfriend.

Approximately forty students and several teachers mill around the school lobby, uncertainly awaiting instructions. Max and I stand among them. The school is asking for help distributing flyers with a description of the missing girl and police contact information. There's hushed excitement evident in the area as under and upperclassmen group together and talk about the fact that another little girl has gone missing.

Max seems okay now, but I practically had to drag him out of the house to get him to come. He kept arguing he couldn't leave, because he's grounded. I finally told him

Mom would be more upset if we didn't help find the daughter of one of her co-workers.

Principal Morris and the school's resource officer walk up to the podium.

"Okay, listen up to uh, Officer Rick Hough." Principal Morris announces with his usual stutter, before he passes an eagle-eye stare across the group to communicate his unwillingness to put up with much. Still, one girl lets out a quickly silenced nervous giggle.

"Thank you, sir. I appreciate all of you coming down. Our town needs all of the eyes and ears we can get to help bring Melissa Cotton home safely. I'm sure there are many rumors going to fly about her disappearance, but we are here to focus on what we can do to get the word out about her and bring her home. Hopefully."

Hopefully? That doesn't sound promising.

A girl standing the front near Max blurts out, "What if she wandered off and is lost in the woods or somewhere and can't find her way home?" Every face in the common area turns to look at her and she finishes weakly, "You know, like in the Little Red Riding Hood story."

"That was Goldilocks," Max says. "Little Red Riding Hood already knew her way to the grandma's house."

Way to go, Mr. Literal. His comments cause some snickers, but nobody has the nerve to laugh out loud with Principal Morris and a policeman standing there. Thank goodness Principal Morris has been around Max enough by now to understand his personality quirk of saying the obvious even when it isn't socially acceptable. He shakes his head at Max and eagle eyes the rest of us attempting to quell further comments.

"Do the police think this is the same guy who took that little Mexican girl and threw her body in the river?" a senior named Darrin asks, reminding us just how bad this situation has the potential to turn out. "Shouldn't we all head down to the ponds or creeks or river instead of going around to houses and businesses?"

Way to voice the belief many of us have, and I see several nod in agreement. Principal Morris walks toward to Devin, but Officer Hough waves him off.

"At this point there's no reason to believe her disappearance and any of the deaths are related. The trained professionals will follow all leads wherever they feel it is appropriate to investigate. Your only task is to get these flyers into the hands of Madison's townspeople."

"All of you just ne, ne, need to do what you're told." Principal Morris has to put in his uh, two cents.

The group bristles at his words and tone. Ordering teenagers to do what they're told is not a good method for motivating them. Officer Hough seems to understand this.

"Let me rephrase what your principal has said. I know you have questions and there will be answers, but right now we need to get the word out about her. You are the best group to get this done quickly." Officer Hough looks around trying to determine if we support this. Once he sees a few heads nod affirmatively, he continues, "So remember, everyone stays with their partners at all times. If a place looks questionable, don't go there. Nobody goes into houses or gets in cars. Are there any questions about these instructions?"

The only sound is the distant repetitive *whirr* of the office copiers still running off flyers.

"Good. We already have one missing person and we don't need any others. In a moment I will dismiss you to pick your partner. Not now!" Officer Hough shouts as everyone immediately starting calling dibs on partners. People stop. Mostly.

"As I was saying, after I release you and you get a partner, be sure to line up at those back tables. MHS staff is waiting with flyers, the needed supplies to hang them, and your location assignments. Questions? None? You are dismissed."

Chaos ensues as people grab at others to claim partners and rush for their supplies.

Max seems eager to make up for his earlier faux pas Goldilocks comment by showing he's trying to be responsible. He turns toward me, "You want me to go get the flyers?"

"Yeah, I want see if Kayla came in."

Max hurries away and I make my way through some of the students to the entrance. Alyssa and Jenna from the dance team are here, but I can't find Kayla anywhere. Where is she this morning? Maybe Cindy came home and they decided to drive her to an alcohol rehabilitation facility. It's happened before.

I pass by Claire, but don't stop to say anything. She's standing in line with a girl from our math class and seeing her reminds me of the flyer about the self-defense classes. Today's events make me wish I would have done more to help than give Mom the flyer. I don't even want to think about Kayla's response if another kid dies. I'll have to worry about that later, because Max comes up with the flyers, an industrial stapler, and our location assignment.

"I'm thirsty. We don't have that many flyers left. Let's stop at the Git It an' Git store and buy some drinks. I've got money." Max indicates the front pocket of his jeans before he wipes his face with the sleeve of his shirt.

We do only have a few flyers left to post and we've covered most of the area to the west of what Madison calls downtown business area. It is surprisingly tiring and hard to get staples to stick in the hard wood of the signposts and telephone poles that mostly make up our assigned area. Our hands hurt now, so we've been taking turns holding the flyers and operating the staple gun. Another twenty feet or so and we'll be on the main drag where the fair booths are being reopened for tonight's action.

"Let's finish this block first."

It's my turn to staple, and as he holds up a flyer, I notice the black that still decorates Max's hand. "So, what's the deal with your hand? What were you up to last night?"

Max closes his eyes. "Can you keep a secret?"

"I never ratted you out to Mom for breaking her Christmas angel snow globe. She still thinks Thor knocked it off the tree with his tail."

Max is quiet until the last staple is inserted on this flyer and we walk toward the next pole.

"Okay, but you can't tell..." We both jump at the sudden sound of a siren. "Hey, what's going on?" Max asks.

A Madison police car is barreling down the street toward us at a high rate of speed. A really high rate of speed, considering the street ahead is full of fair vendors and other people.

The police officer shouts orders through his megaphone. "Clear the street! Clear the street! You, with the cart. Move! Move!"

The car slides in a ninety degree turn around the Rotary Club's Bingo tent and clips one of the metal tent stakes with a loud *ping* before it screeches to a stop. Multiple other sirens in the distance are coming in fast. Max drops the flyers to the ground and I drop the heavy stapler on top to secure them. By the time we reach the corner, the news comes rolling back from the growing crowd like a destructive tidal wave that won't be stopped. Seems our time and efforts hanging flyers to help find the little girl have been a waste.

Melissa Cotton floats face down in the Senior Class Fundraiser dunking tank.

Seven weeks later and that little Cotton girl's killer is still not behind bars. Just a crying shame and a poor use of our tax dollars, too.

History teacher up at the high school was the one that found the poor little thing. He was a'helping the Senior Class set up for the fair and pulled that tarp off and there she was. Drowned right in the dunking machine.

When Gladys called to tell me about little Melissa, now the Lord's newest angel, being called home, I said, "Lock your doors, Gladys. Them devil-worshipping carnival folks is gonna kill us all!"

Then I read in the paper that the same night the girl was taken, there was some of them evil-doers were over at the park just a tearing things up and a spray-paintin' their devil signs and profanity all over everything. I figured it to be more of the same bunch.

I say someone ought to call in one of the forensic teams like them television shows. Those special detectives always get their man and they can get it done in less than an hour.

Florence Cobb-Concerned Citizen

15

The clanging noise that accompanies the closing of my locker sounds unusually loud in the nearly empty hallway. It's about twenty minutes after last bell, but only a few people remain at school. It *is* the Wednesday before Thanksgiving break. Even most of the teachers are clearing out. My science teacher hadn't needed much help with the class water samples, so I can get home and chill until tomorrow's turkey dinner. I don't even have much homework. Just a couple of scenes from Julius Caesar that we ended up reading anyway. Sure hope nobody dies. Bad joke, since I already know the ending. But this town has seen enough of death recently. It's all anyone seems to focus on.

"Hi, Marty."

Claire's voice from behind me surprises me. I turn, with a smile ready for her. Kayla's still my number one girl, but it's been nice to have another friend who's a girl. You can always count on them to smell a lot better than guy friends.

"Hey, Claire. What're you still doing here?"

"I was talking with Miss Brandel about our story." Claire and I have been working on a story for the school newspaper about all of the different programs taking place in the community to keep the local kids safer. Kayla isn't happy about our working together in this class too, but the teacher claims it's good for people to branch out with other partners.

"What about it?"

"She suggests we might do an investigative summary for the high school students of what the police actually know. You know, to help cut down on the rumors." Claire shifts her heavy bag over to her other shoulder. I know from talking with her in math that the bag is most likely full of the suspense books she likes to read.

"I'd think there's enough of those stories already on the news. Every station from Kansas City has a special investigative team interviewing people all over town. People in town are already so stirred up about what happened, Billy said a little kid at his church tried to turn him in for stranger danger when he passed around the collection plate last Sunday."

The light in Claire's eyes dim a little at the sarcastic tone of my comments. I hurry to say something that will bring some of the brightness back.

"But if you think it's a good idea, I'm willing to work with you on it."

"Great." Claire smiles and adds, "We don't have to use that horrid name for the crimes that idiotic reporter came up with. I want our article to be respectful of the families."

I want to respect those families too. Their daughters are dead and even now weeks later they can barely step outside their houses without being bombarded with reporters trying to get an exclusive comment. Max's friend, Jacob, is so bad now with all that is going on, he hardly comes to school. If anyone speaks to him at all, whether it's friends, teachers, or even administrators, he just turns and walks out the front door. I don't know where he goes after that and I don't think his parents do, either. They call our house sometimes at night looking for him.

"Agreed. No sensational *Floating Angels Murders* headlines. Only hard facts for this investigative team."

"Thanks, Marty. Right now, we've got their names and locations where they were found. I'll see what I can gather up for information this weekend. Maybe we'll find something to connect the crimes."

"That would be something. I'll write down some ideas of who we might interview."

"We can do it together after break." Claire's usual smile gives way to a sudden pink flush on her cheeks. "I mean we can start work on the article after break."

Crud. Does Claire like me? She's pretty hot in a quirky girl kind of way, but Kayla is not going to be cool with this. I am saved from making a response when Alyssa bounces up. She stares suspiciously at Claire and ignores her as she tells me to have good break with Kayla, stress on the name of my girlfriend.

"Later, Marty." Claire heads for the front door. The smile now missing from her face and quick exit prove she isn't willing to be treated poorly by Alyssa, or most likely anyone else.

I frown as I say goodbye. I wish I could follow and talk some more, but it's in everyone's best interests to let Claire go. Alyssa would report it to Kayla and girls can be mean.

I look over at Alyssa watching me like one of those carrion birds waiting for road kill scraps. I let loose with a little of my own meanness.

"So Alyssa, try not to run into a tree when you are in Colorado this year." Her family is loaded. Everyone knows about their annual skiing trips over Thanksgiving break and that Alyssa often comes home on crutches.

"Hey!" Alyssa protests, "I only did that once. That tree popped up out of nowhere."

"Once?" I know better.

"Okay, twice. Quit picking on me." She huffs and starts off toward the back of the building. "I just came back to get my iPod from my gym bag. Can't stand my family all the way across Kansas without it. Bye."

I don't even wave.

When I close my locker and pick up my backpack, I think about Alyssa's protectiveness. It could be a good thing that someone thinks my relationship with Kayla is worth fighting for, because there are a lot of days I wonder. Ever since the fair and the night we met up with Cindy and Snake, the relationship has gone nowhere. Kayla and I still hold hands and kiss and other stuff sometimes, but Kayla is distracted and seems kind of uninterested in us. In me. Definite ego-killer.

Things have been so bad between us, I even ask Mom for advice. She reminds me that Cindy has been at rehab since the fair and to be patient with Kayla. I'm trying, but I suck at being patient. I hope things will be better after tomorrow. Cindy is getting a pass for the day and Kayla's family is coming over for Thanksgiving dinner.

"Marty. Marty!"

My hand reaches to push on the outside door, but turn around when I heard my journalism teacher Miss Brandel calling my name.

She jogs up to me, her lanyard with school ID card and a collection of other crap flying up and down wildly and threatening to take out an eye with every bounce.

"I'm so glad you're still here. I was afraid I would have to wait until I got back from Chicago to call you," she announces, puffing a bit from exertion.

"Chicago sounds cool. I've never been." I offer these comments to give her a chance to catch her breath.

"You're probably smarter. The airports are atrocious."

Atrocious is a good college vocabulary builder.

"I'll have to take your word, Miss Brandel. I've never flown before."

"You will one day," she assures me. "I have great faith that your writing and photography skills will take you far. Don't try Jeff's method of flight though."

I smile. "I won't. Thanks for the compliments. I really like being on the staff."

"You should. You're good. That is what I want to talk to you about."

I look at her quizzically.

"I was down at the local paper, The Madison Chronicle, to pick up some yearbook proof sheets, and one of their reporters, Cy Hanover, asked me if I had a high school student who might be interested in doing a paid internship. He needs someone with writing ability and who will be responsible. I thought of you immediately. Are you interested?" Miss Brandel seems excited for me.

"I guess. What would I be doing for him?"

"Probably run errands at first or take notes at some meetings in town. He's the one who's been doing all of the local pieces on the girls. I've heard you talk about that little Peterson girl in class, so I know you have some interest."

Not more of the murders! I open my mouth to turn the opportunity down when she continues.

"You'll make a decent salary and the last intern was going to events and publishing photos and articles on his own before he got a full time job at another paper."

"I'm interested. But wouldn't I need to be able to drive? I can't even take my test until March."

"Oh, I don't think you would need to drive. The office is on the corner of Bates and Third. Isn't that close enough to your house to walk?"

"Yes." And it was. A real reporter at a real newspaper who got paid? Add what Max and I already made with Twin Cuts, his salary from the activity center, and what I would get paid, and we should be able to buy insurance and maybe even our own car. I could take Kayla on a real date. We could go parking and make out without somebody interrupting us all the time. That would probably make things better between us.

"This sounds great. Thank you, Miss Brandel!" I experience such a moment of joy and exuberance at all of the possibilities of this opportunity that I hug her.

Hug? A teacher? In public?

Crap! I may have to turn in my standoffish surly teen-ager card.

Miss Brandel and I look at each other in shock for a second until I quickly step away from her. She smiles goofily. I didn't need to see myself in the reflection of the school's front door to know I am glowing red from embarrassment from the edge of my dark hair to the tips of my size twelve feet.

Miss Brandel gives me a few seconds to recover by ripping out a piece of paper from the tiny notepad and pen set she has attached to her lanyard.

"Uh…you're welcome. Marty. Let me just jot down Mr. Hanover's full name and the address of the newspaper office. You'll need to go in Monday afternoon for an interview. He's a little gruff, so try not to be put off by that.

I grab the paper and mumble another thanks and turn to leave before I can do something else embarrassing.

Miss Brandel calls after me and I can hear the effort she's making not to laugh openly. "Marty Jamison, you just made my day! Have a great holiday."

I utter something that sounds polite and burst out the door.

Great job offer or not, I just hugged a woman who is out of college. She may even be close to twenty-five. Maybe thirty!

Gross.

Hi, hon.

No, there's not much going on in town. Lot of cars still out with everyone heading out for the big family dinners. I'm gonna do one more run through town. Then I'll stop by for my break.

My mouth is already watering for that turkey I smelled when I went out the door this morning. Can't wait for the dressing and some sweet...wait, what is that kid doin'? I've got to go, hon. Keep a plate warm.

Hey! Hey, you. Stop right there!

Stan Boyer-Madison Patrolman

16

"And we are grateful for all of this food placed before us and for the family and friends seated at our table and those who can't be with us. Amen." Mom ends the annual prayer of the Thanksgiving meal.

"Amen," everyone echoes.

Max plops the first of numerous spoonful's of mashed potatoes on his plate and I have two warm homemade rolls in one hand and am reaching for a turkey leg when Mom screeches, "Hold it right there, you two. We all haven't shared what we are thankful for this year.

Max whines like a little girl, "Please, Mom!"

My own, "Please, Mom!" completes our juvenile whining duet.

Max and I are seated opposite of each other with Mom at one end of the dining room table. We are as dressed up as we ever get, in collared shirts and slacks. Thanksgiving is the one holiday when we really do it up. Mom, Cindy, Susan and Kayla have all made an extra effort to look nice too. Kayla looks especially good in a short blue dress that makes her legs look super long. I plan to tell her later just how good, but now all I think about is digging into all of this food.

My cohort in attempted coercion, Max, joins me in combining our guilt-trip powers to stare Mom down by employing matching puppy dog eyes and pouty lips.

Susan laughs while making a plea for us, "Maybe we better let these growing boys dig in or they might start gnawing the table legs of this beautiful antique oak table."

Mom groans. "Aren't they just shameless? You would think they both hadn't eaten a bowl of cereal this morning while I was busy slaving over this meal!"

Max and I know we've won the battle, but Max clarifies, "It wasn't just one bowl."

"It was two!" I chime in with my line.

Together we lean up from our chairs and reach across the turkey to pound it out as we finish, "Each!"

Mom tries to keep a frown on her face, but breaks up as everyone else at the table laughs.

We are a happy group today. My family and Kayla and her mom and aunt have been celebrating this holiday together for years and we look forward to it. Even Cindy, who's here from the rehab center and looks a little shaky today, seems to be enjoying herself. The only usual dinner participant not seated and laughing with us at the table is Thor. He waits patiently near Mom's seat, ever watchful for dropped crumbs or handouts.

We all watch Mom in anticipation of the official signal to eat. She places her napkin daintily in her lap. "We can wait until after we eat to share what we are thankful for."

Max and I scream an enthusiastic yes, but before we could grab any food she continues in a serious tone, "Before we begin, I want to remind everyone *not* to feed Thor any of the deviled eggs. I think we all recall how that turned out."

The group nods their heads in agreement. The effect of those eggs on our dog's digestive system isn't something anyone would forget easily. Thor doesn't even have the decency to look embarrassed.

"My second announcement is—go!"

Mom snags a spoonful of Max's potatoes and one of my rolls before either of us can move. Mary Jo Jamison, woman extraordinaire has beaten us at our own food grabbing game. The next thirty minutes in our dining room is full of happy conversation and the sounds of people enjoying delicious food. I gorge on multiple helpings of all my favorites and am debating whether it was too early to ask for pie, when I catch Kayla smiling at me. I smile back.

Today, she looks more like the old Kayla. Her hair is all smooth and glossy, her smile's genuine, and it seems that having her mom here for the day makes my girlfriend happier. Works for me. Maybe after dinner we can sneak a kiss or two. Or more.

Ding, ding, ding. Max and I groan in unison at the sound of Mom tapping her butter knife on her nearly empty glass of iced tea.

"Now that we have decimated this Thanksgiving dinner, I would like to hear what everyone is thankful for this holiday," Mom orders. "Who would like to begin?"

Complete silence.

"Okay, I will begin. I am grateful I had a working oven again this year."

Everyone giggles, because one year, our oven broke and we ate chili for the Thanksgiving meal. It was good chili, but it hadn't measured up to today's food.

Susan goes next. "I am grateful for the opportunity to have all of my family and friends here together."

"Here, here!" Max says in a fake British accent.

We turn to stare at him. Then we all laugh at once.

"What? I saw it on television," he says sheepishly. "It was one of those documentary things."

We giggle some more and Cindy speaks next. She says hesitantly, "I am thankful for good friends and family, who..." She takes a deep breath, "who never let me down the way I sometimes let them down."

"Oh, Cindy, we all love you," Susan says as she reaches over and pats her sister's arm.

"Here, here!" Max says again and sets everyone to giggling so loudly we wake Thor from where he's resting, post dinner handouts.

"Kayla, what about you?" Mom asks. "What are you thankful for this year?"

Kayla bows her head for a moment, then looks up at me and says, "I'm grateful for all the people who try to be there for others." She smiles over at her mom.

"That's a lovely one, dear," Mom praises and looks at me next.

I debate on saying something serious to show my sensitive, deeper side to impress the ladies present, but go with my truth instead. "I'm grateful for pumpkin pie with extra whipped topping that my mom is about to go into the kitchen and get for me."

Mom smacks at me with her napkin and shrieks, "Martin Joseph Jamison!"

Max calls me a piehead. Everyone else howls with laughter and in the middle of this Thor suddenly lets out a huge fart. Everyone is silent for a moment and then we all start pulling our shirts or napkins up over our mouths and noses. Max is given the job of relocating Thor to the utility room while Mom jokingly tries to interrogate those of us at the table to determine who gave the dog one of the deviled eggs. Mom fixes her eyes on Max when he returns to the table. "It's your turn to share what you're thankful for this year. And I don't want to hear one word like your brother's comment."

Max smirks at me, but begins solemnly. "I am thankful for the women who prepared this good food—"

Those women nod their heads in approval.

"And that those women will be the ones washing all of the dishes while we men eat our pie and take a nap."

Cries of laughing outrage and napkins rain down on both of us as I high five Maxwell James Jamison, my twin, and now officially known as one of my favorite people.

Kayla and I break our mouths apart, both of us gasping for breath. Post dinner departures of Susan to drive Cindy back to the rehabilitation center and of Mom and Max to walk Thor have provided us time to talk and make out. Talking took only a minute and now we are enjoying the making out portion with enthusiasm.

Kayla sits up. I go in for another tonsil licking kiss when Kayla interrupts my move with a question. "Don't you think we better stop? How long does it usually take to walk Thor?"

"Depends." I move forward, still intent on my lip lock target.

"On?" She leans back.

I sigh and sit up fully.

"On how cold it is. They will coming back soon. We better quit." I say this as reluctantly as anything I've ever said in my life. I sure hope I get that job on Monday, because I really want to buy a car for dating.

I look at Kayla to see how she's taking the news. She looks so fantastic right now. Her long hair is all down around her face and her bow lies on the coffee table. Her lips are puffy from our kissing. The top of Kayla's blue dress is hanging low on her chest and the bottom's riding high on the thighs of her long, gorgeous legs. I can't see what my hair, face, and clothes look like, but she looks like we have been doing exactly what we've been doing. Even the fact that her jawline is red from where my tiny whiskers stick out from my morning's shave doesn't make me want to stop from going in for another kiss. I lean in for it only to be thwarted when the door from the utility room slams open.

"Max, please just calm down. I will call Jacob's mom and find out how he's doing," Mom calls loudly from the kitchen.

Max stomps past the doorway to the living room and down the hall.

"How's a phone call going to help my best friend get out of jail?" Max yells back over his shoulder before rushing into our bedroom.

Slam! The whole wall of photos hanging above the couch rattles before settling back in a newly crooked order. Kayla and I stare at each other wondering what set Max off.

"Mom?" I say and am only slightly embarrassed when my voice cracks a little.

She comes slowly around the corner into the living room. Her face is red from the cold, but kind of pinched too.

"It's Jacob. He's been arrested. Their neighbors said an officer saw him committing a crime, but he ran off. Someone in the neighbor recognized him running by, identified him to the officer, and two squad cars were at his house picking him up when we walked by."

"*Ja-cob* got arrested?" Even though both Max and Mom said it, I can't believe it.

"Yes, but he's still fifteen, isn't he? So he'll go to the Juvenile Detention Center. I think."

"What did he do?" Kayla asks.

"Vandalism. They think he and some other kids have been the ones tagging with spray paint all over town and tearing up the park. The police said they won't stop until they have all the vandals in custody."

"How did Max handle seeing the police take him into custody?" I remember what happens when someone is mean to Jacob in front of my brother. "Was he okay?"

Mom nods. "He was—is upset, but he was okay. Kayla, could you gather up your stuff so I can run you home?" She looks at me. "Marty, you'll have to stay."

I would rather ride along, but I'll be here with Max. It's no wonder he's upset. Wow. Best friend in jail for some clearly bad behavior.

I feel a whole lot better about what Kayla and I have been up to on Mom's sofa.

It's been pretty quiet since the fair. I almost messed that up big time. I didn't have time to find a more secluded spot, and I couldn't wait. It wasn't right of her mom to treat her like that. It wasn't. She needed help. So I did it.

The press is using the name, "floating angels" and I think it fits my girls. They do look like angels when I help them find peace from all of their problems.

That's a good thing, right?

The Killer

17

"You okay?" I ask Max about twenty minutes later when it becomes apparent he intends to ignore me. I'm in our bedroom to change out of my dress clothes, but I'm really there to check on him.

"I guess." Max answers as I pull on some sweats. His voice is muffled as he lies on his side on his bed facing away from me. "Mom taking Kayla home?"

"Yeah." I roll up my slacks and shoot them toward the basket that serves as a clothes hamper. Score!

"Lucky you. Stuck babysitting your bipolar brother again." Max's voice rings with bitterness. It's true, but I'm not going to point it out when he's having a bad time.

"Mom told me what happened with Jacob. Getting arrested for tagging and vandalism sucks."

"Sure does."

Max sounds resigned. This is weird. Normally, he'd be all hyped up and full of ideas to help his friend out.

I disguise my worry by ruffling through one of my drawers, taking out tee shirts and smelling them to find one that's relatively clean. Mom will throw a fit if she ever realizes just how often Max and I shove dirty clothes into dresser instead of our hamper. I find a shirt that isn't too funky from too much teen body odor.

Before I can pull the shirt over my head, Max rolls over and sits up on the side of his bed. "I need to tell you something I did. Something bad."

I sit down on my own bed and the shirt falls to the floor. I decide I'm still too full to bother with picking it up and I want hear what my brother has to say. He says nothing.

"Max?"

"You have to promise not to tell Mom."

"Okay." I have to know now.

"Marty, you remember the night of the fair when I got grounded?" Max begins rocking back and forth.

"Yeah, when we all rode the rides and then the next day they found that last little dead girl." I have no clue where Max is going with this and his rocking is freaking me out. "Please stop that."

Max stops. He looks grim. "Later that night I saw Jacob …and he was…he had…"

A horrific possibility comes to me.

"Wait! Jacob Peterson didn't…He didn't kill those little girls, did he? Even Natalee? That's his freakin' sister!" I'm practically incoherent at the possibility that someone I actually know might have been crazy enough to kill all those little girls. Or anyone, for that matter.

"No! Not that! Jacob wouldn't do that."

Max and I both jump off our beds and stand facing each other. His fists ball up. His facial expression indicates he wants to punch me in the head now. Hard.

"Crap, Marty. How can you even think something like that? He's been our friend for years."

"Then *what* are you trying to tell me?"

Max takes a deep breath and unclenches his fists. "Jacob didn't kill anybody, but he was tagging and vandalizing stuff like the cops said."

"That's not good, but it's not that bad." I am relieved.

"I know. But there's more," Max says and then I am not relieved.

Max sits on his bed and motions for me to sit down too.

I leave the shirt on the floor where it fell.

"You remember that day during the fair when we were hanging flyers?" Max isn't hiding his face now—his eyes drill into my own. "You asked me about the black stuff on my hand?"

"Yeah. I remember." My forehead crinkles in between my eyebrows as I try to make sense of what this has to do with Jacob getting arrested.

"That stuff on my hand was paint, because I was with Jacob that night. I was tagging in the park too." Max studies my face waiting for a reaction.

It's simple. I'm shocked.

Max, tagging? Spraying graffiti all over buildings? No way. He's more the kind of guy to paint over and fix the things other people deface. The blood rushes into my head when I realize he hasn't even told me about this until now.

"Why, Max?"

"Because I was being stupid. I was mad. Everybody else kept leaving me that night. Ray and Billy left to go drink at a party. You were off with Kayla again. I ran into Jacob on my way home. He hadn't been talking to me for weeks, but he acted like he was glad to see me and wanted us to hang out together." He rubs his hands back and forth on the jeans he changed into before taking Thor on the walk with Mom.

I am a jerk. And selfish, too. I had been so caught up in trying to make Kayla happy, I'd forgotten that for Max, I was his best friend too. With Jacob in and out of the picture, my brother had been lonely and all too happy to do whatever his old buddy said to get someone to hang out with.

"What happened after you went with Jacob?" I might feel guilty, but I want the facts.

"Jacob pulled some spray paint cans out of his hoodie when we got to the park. He handed one to me and we just started tagging tables and trash cans and signs."

"You've been going around and tearing crap up with Jacob? When? You're always at school or your job at the activity center."

"I only tagged that one time and I didn't break any of that stuff they talked about in the paper. We were just painting stuff, but when we got close to the pool, Jacob became crazy and not my kind. He pulled down the chain link fence and broke the windows on the concession stand. I tried to get him to stop." Max repeatedly smacks his thighs with his hands.

"Stop!" I order. "Now go on." Since Max's opened up to me, I want to hear the rest.

"He starts punching the cement blocks on the building over and over. He won't listen when I tell him to stop. His hands are bleeding and that's when he starts hitting his head on the wall. It was horrible. Just *Thunk, thunk, thunk!* Over and over." Max takes a deep shuddering breath. "I got up and pushed him away from the wall. Then he picked up a loose board and kept swinging it at my head. Said he was going to kill me if I didn't leave. He looked like he meant it. I ran to the trees at the edge of the park and hid in brush where I could watch him."

"What'd he do next?"

"Waited until he thought I was gone and sat down and cried. After a while he got up and walked home. I followed him and stayed until he went inside."

"That's why you were so late," I state.

"Well, I couldn't tell Mom the truth. I couldn't rat out my friend and Mom would have lost it when she heard what I did."

"No kidding." I nod my head in agreement concerning Mom's reaction. The major reason that Max and I don't get in more trouble often is because we can't stand to disappoint her. She's had enough of that with Dad.

"I knew Jacob needed help and I went to talk to him that next night after the little girl was found in the dunking tank. He's been hiding out in his room all day, because his parents didn't act like they'd seen his cuts and bruises. Jacob didn't know another girl died until I told him. He got real quiet and then begged me not to tell anyone about the park. He said he was sorry about trying to hit me. I made him promise me he wouldn't hurt himself or tag or tear anything else up."

Max wrings his hands. "I believed him, Marty. At first. But then I kept seeing his mark with his initials in a bunch of places all over town. I tried to ask him about it a few weeks ago and he told me to keep my mouth shut. Now he won't talk to me at all." Max keeps wringing his hands in the silence until I reach over to grab them. "That night I really thought he was going to keep bashing his head against the wall until he died."

"You really think he would have?"

Max looks up into my eyes. "Maybe. But I knew I couldn't take someone else trying to kill themselves and not do anything to stop them. Not again."

I take a deep breath as I realize that there's a lot more to my brother than I ever give him credit for. That anyone gives him credit for. He deserves better from us. From me.

"Max, next time you can tell me serious crap like this. Or even tell Mom. We'd help you. You shouldn't be worrying about this kind of stuff. It's not good for you."

Max abruptly slides back across his bed, putting his back against the wall and snaps at me. "You mean because I'm bipolar. That I shouldn't worry because I might get depressed and end up like Dad. Sometimes you and Mom make me so mad!" Max crosses his arms, glaring across at me. "I'm not Dad. I listen to the doctor and take all of the medicine, so I can manage my stress just fine. Being B.P. doesn't automatically mean that I am the weak twin or that I need you to come in and save the day!"

When did my little brother become this guy? The guy who's right.

"I'm sorry, Max. You're a good friend to Jacob. You kept the secret to give him the time to come up with a better way to grieve. It might not have worked, but you tried." I swallow. "Next time though, you need to tell me what's going on, so I can come up with a plan to fix the problem."

Max stares at me, saying nothing. Oh crud, I am doing it again.

"I'm sorry. I know Mom and I are too protective, but we're family and we don't want to fail you. I don't think either of us can take it if we fail you."

Still nothing.

"Okay, I'll work it, little brother," I grin. "But good luck trying to convince Mom to back off. Not even a crowbar will make a dent in her determination to care for us."

Max can't help his own grin and uncrosses his arms. His face and body relax and his eyes light up when he nods toward my shirt still lying on the floor beside the bed.

"Then there's one other important thing I need to tell you."

"What is it?" I steel myself to accept whatever Max is going to say next.

"You sure you won't run to Mom? It's the kind of thing that will make her want to give the *sex talk* again. "

The one where she sat both of us down and explained the mechanics of the act and how both partners should treat each other with respect. I don't have a clue what Max is about to tell me, but it can't be as horrifyingly embarrassing as my mother's lecture.

"Go ahead and tell me, Max. I won't say anything. Promise."

"You really need to put your shirt on."

"Why?" I glance down at my bare chest and then over where Max is grinning widely.

"Kayla gave you a present." He gestures toward the mirror over the chest of drawers.

I jump up and look in the mirror, mystified, until I see the big round purple hickey.

"Impressive." I gently rub the spot just under my collarbone. "I didn't even notice her doing it."

"Well, Mom will notice it, if you don't cover it up."

I catch Max's gaze in the mirror. "Thanks, man."

"You know me, always wanting to help my big brother out."

Had a call this week from a couple of kids from the high school. They're doing an article for their paper on Floating Angels Murders and wanted to know if there was anything new to report. I told them no.

I couldn't tell them if there was, but it's the first week of December and two full months since that Cotton girl was pulled out of the tank. We've got nothing on her murder or a link from the other dead girls to it. We interviewed everyone even remotely connected, reviewed what little forensic evidence there was, and the only patterns we've been able to determine are that all of the girls are between six and eight and they lived here in Madison.

There isn't much to say at this point. For now we all wait and hope the killer stops on his own.

Unfortunately, in my experience that doesn't happen much.

C. Ashe-Chief Investigator

18

"You any good with a computer?"

"Yes, Mr. Hanover. I'm not a super fast typist, but I got an A in keyboarding in middle school." No response from the man peering over his glasses on the other side of the desk, so I add, "And I use the computers at the library during the summer."

"Young man like yourself ought to be outside in the summer, working a real job in the heat and sweating. Not lazing around in some air conditioned building," comes a crotchety retort.

"Uh, well, my brother and I did work outside during the summer too. We have our own mowing and landscaping business. Twin Cuts? We run our ads in this newspaper sometimes." My voice croaks a little on *sometimes.*

I'm trying to survive the hardest interview I'd been on in my life. It's the only interview I've ever been on, but Cy Hanover, the chief investigative reporter of the Madison Chronicle, isn't gruff, like Ms. Brandel said. This guy is old school tough and maybe a little mean. He's already ridiculed what I'm learning in my classes and doesn't seem that impressed by the copies of articles I brought as samples of my work. Even the article Claire and I did summing up the murders. Wonder what I'd have to write to impress this kind of guy? An entire set of encyclopedias like from the library maybe.

All I am sure about is that this man is intimidating. Even at over sixty, he's a big guy, and not in a fat way. He doesn't look like he sat at a desk most of his life. He looks more like he used to bench press desks. But Cyrus L. Hanover, known professionally as Cy Hanover, must be a good reporter. There are plenty of official looking plaques hanging up on one wall. On another one are framed photos of him and some regular looking people and a few famous ones too. I don't have time to study the walls, because I am watching the man searching for something by patting the numerous piles of papers covering his desk.

"You smoke, Jamison?"

"Smoke?" I repeat.

"Yeah, smoke. You know, cigarettes?" He stops his desktop pat down to stare intently at me. "Or maybe something else?"

"No." Is this old guy asking if I smoke weed? "I don't smoke anything. At all." My face reddens even though I really haven't.

Cy nods his head in an affirmative. "Well don't start. My niece and the doc been on to me to quit. Got me chewing that nicotine gum."

"That's nice, sir." Nice? Could I sound like any more of a suck up?

Mr. Hanover looks at me over his glasses. I can tell he thinks I sound like a suck up too.

"I just never can find that gum when I need it. Help search," he orders before going into a wheezy coughing fit letting me know he *really* shouldn't smoke.

I lean forward and carefully began sifting through what look like haphazard piles of lists and letters and articles. I figure he'll be the kind of guy to fire me before I even get hired if I mess up his papers.

I try to make conversation while we search. "It's nice that your family and doctor care about your health, sir." Here I go again. Suck.

"I suppose. You got family? You a Momma's or Daddy's boy?"

I'm not sure I want to answer that last part. I am a Momma's boy, but that seems logical under the circumstances. "My father passed away several years ago. My mom's a nurse at the hospital and I have a twin brother."

"Twin, huh? You the kind that look alike?"

"Yes, sir. Most people can't tell us apart when they see us or even when we're talking on the phone. We're mirror image twins, so we're identical, but I'm right-handed and my brother Max is left-handed." Why did I say that last part?

Mr. Hanover rolls his chair back and motions for me to keep looking. Pretty soon he asks me a question I've been dreading.

"Your dad used to be the Jamison that owned the garage over on Beecher Street?"

Great, if the man knows that, he knows Dad offed himself there too. Probably wrote a story about it. This interview is over if Mr. Hanover is the kind of man who's leery of hiring the son of the guy who couldn't deal with his problems. I nod, afraid to say anything.

After a moment, Mr. Hanover gestures up toward the pictures above his head.

"I served over in Nam. Worked for Army's press corps writing articles and taking pictures. That's me hanging out of the chopper." He indicates an 8 X 10 black and white photo to his left.

I look at the photo and nod again. It's impressive.

"Met some great fellas out in those jungles. Good men. Not all of them made it back." Mr. Hanover is quiet for a moment. "Plenty of the ones who got home couldn't take the stress of living in a country that seemed to hate 'em for doing what Uncle Sam had told 'em was their jobs. A lot lost their way and then we lost them too. Like I said, good men." He stares down at the floor.

Mr. Hanover doesn't appear to remember I'm here and after a minute of quietly waiting for him to speak again, I start searching through his papers again. I look up when he rolls his chair up to his desk, pulls out his center drawer and pops a piece of gum out of the pack that must have been in there the whole time. He motions me to sit back from the desk.

I sit there, confused and wondering if the man suffered a head injury during the war or if he's simply senile. The only sound in the office for the next minute is the pop of Mr. Hanover's gum. His next question startles me. "Is your momma a good looking gal?"

"What? I, uh, I guess." Great, now I was stuttering like Principal Morris. My eyebrows jump into a "V" trying to understand why this matters.

"I'll bet she's real lonely without a man. Think she'd like it if I stopped by and offered to do a little Hanover Hustle with her?"

Did I hear that correctly? Did Mr. Cy Hanover, award winning veteran reporter, just make a lewd suggestion involving my mother, Mary Jo Jamison? This is not okay. Can he even ask crap like this? In an interview?

Screw this old geezer! There isn't a job in the world where I'm willing to listen to that kind of comment concerning Mom.

I jump up and my body and voice both shake as I begin, "Sir, nobody talks about my mother like that. You can go straight to—"

Hanover fly's up out of his chair in a move pretty spry for a wheezy old guy. "You're hired, Jamison! Any man that will stand up for his blessed mother has the kind of integrity I expect in an employee." He extends his hand for a shake.

I ignore it. This isn't over.

"Now son, I was just rattling your cage a little. You stop by Marge on your way out to get your paperwork, so you can start getting paid for putting up with the likes of me." He extends his hand further.

Not good enough, Geezer! I have this guy figured out. When I clasp his hand in my own, I squeeze tightly in my best attempt at a bone-crunching grasp. First, I thank him for the job. Then, I explain as forcefully as I've ever said anything in my life that he is never to speak like that about my mother again. Ever. I smile, release his hand, and stand up straight.

Mr. Hanover looks me over and tries one more time to buffalo me into submission. He stands up to his considerable full height. "You think you can take me, son?"

I lean across his desk with my face as close to his as I can get it. I'm only up to his chin, but I don't let it stop me. "No sir, I don't. By *myself*," I pause for emphasis, "but there's another one at home just like me. *Together*...we can make you regret the day you ever disrespected *our* mom."

Mr. Hanover is dead silent. Then he barks out a loud and deep laugh followed by some belly-busting guffaws that end in raspy smoker's coughs. When he can breathe again, Mr. Hanover says, "Boy, you can call me Cy."

"Mr. Hanover will be fine, sir."

Cough, cough, cough. The man dots his mouth with the handkerchief he removes from his pocket.

"You'll do, young man. Now get out of here Jamison, 'fore you kill me." *Cough.* "Another one at home just like you..."

Ho, ho, ho. Come here little girl and sit on Santa's lap. What's her name, Momma?

Victoria. That's a pretty name. Now tell Santa what you want for Christmas.

What? You want your daddy to stop being so mean, because it makes you sad? Oh don't worry about it, Momma. Kids say all kinds of things up here.

Veronica, how about Santa brings you a new doll or a baking oven instead? You'd like that, wouldn't you, Veronica? What? Sorry, I mean Victoria.

Wayne Ervine-Mall Santa

19

"Do you think Kayla would like something simple like this?" Mom questions, pointing to a couple of gold and silver chains.

"Maybe, but let's keep looking." I gaze across the expanse of glass cases holding the department store's jewelry collection.

At least I'm not the only one who waits until the last minute to buy presents. The mall is full others trying to finish up their Christmas shopping. I don't see anyone else shopping with their mothers, but I'll live down the hit to my cool factor if it helps me get the right gift for Kayla. My mom can provide necessary woman advice and transportation. I can't wait until Max and I have our sixteenth birthdays in a couple of months. The current vehicular dependence will finally become driving freedom.

Max is here at the mall, too. This is one time when I think he's lucky not to have a girlfriend to worry about getting a gift. He suggested buying Kayla socks. No help. Mom sent him down to wait at the food court. Probably he's sucking down a root beer, inhaling nachos, and watching the little babies and toddlers scream when they get a good look at the guy who dresses up as Santa. We both like that and it's more fun than this shopping. I sigh.

"Don't give up yet, Marty." Mom hasn't even looked up to see what's prompted my sigh.

"I haven't." I realize I'm in the engagement and wedding ring section and quickly step to the next one. Kayla and I have been getting along great since Thanksgiving, but not that great.

Mom sees where I have been, "Keep walking, bud. You're too young to be thinking about that and I'm much too young to be a grandmother."

"I know, Mom. I got the message when you gave me the *talk* again last week." I'm joking, but I hadn't done so great at hiding the hickey and that prompted Mom to revisit the talk. "Don't worry nobody's getting married for *any* reason soon."

"Well, good!" Mom taps the glass in front of her. "Marty, since there are so many people in here, I think we should split up."

"Okay. I'll try this side." Heading down the side closest to me, I study a selection of bracelets and squat down to see the price on the impossibly small tags. Man! I make pretty good money working afterschool at the newspaper, but I'd need to work full time and weekends to pay for something like that bracelet. If everything here costs this much, I may just have to go with what I already made her, but I want something special. Like Kayla is to me.

"Hi, Marty."

I look up at Claire. I haven't seen her as much in the weeks since we completed our article outlining the known facts of the drownings. She looks really good tonight. She's kind of dressed up with a black coat and a red scarf and a matching flat hat like on those French shows. Makes her eyes look really pretty. I pretend not to see how much. Not cool to notice another girl when you're Christmas shopping for your girlfriend.

"Hey, Claire. What's up?" My voice cracks at the end. Smooth. I sound like some Nineties boy band member.

She smiles. Either she doesn't notice how dorky I sound or doesn't care. "I'm meeting some of the choir members to perform holiday songs for the shoppers. What's *up* with you?"

She noticed.

"Just shopping. For Kayla. I'm not having much luck." I admit, tapping the glass of the display case.

"Oh." Claire focuses on pulling off her gloves and shoving them in coat pockets. "I'm sure she'll like whatever you give her. I would."

Okay. I'm getting the vibe that Claire likes me again.

"I've got to get going, Marty. I can't be late or they'll only have Jenna Connors to sing the alto part and she's can't stay on pitch. Happy Holidays and all that!"

"You too."

It's a surprise to me that I have to stop myself from giving her a hug. I shake my head to remind me that I'm looking for a present for my girl and nearly walk by the perfect gift.

Resting on a headless neck on the bottom shelf is a silver necklace with a skinny chain that has a curvy initial and tiny diamond sparkling near the top. So far it's the only thing I see that suits Kayla. It's perfect, if the initial is a "K" instead of a disappointing *"D"*.

Mom sidles up beside me where I hunch over the display case. "See anything you like?"

"I do, but they don't have the right initial." I point at the unwanted "D".

"Oh, Marty, you have good taste. I can't wait until you are a rich and famous journalist and can afford to buy me nice jewelry for my gift." Her face lights up like it's already Christmas morning.

I grimace, remembering the boring robe and doggie shaped slippers Max and I bought together before wrapping and putting them under the tree. Maybe she'll light up when she notices that the slippers look like Thor.

Mom giggles at the look on my face and pats my shoulder, "Lighten up, Loverboy! I'm teasing. I think it's sweet that you want to give Kayla some jewelry. Now let's see if we can get a salesperson over here to check for the pendant letter you need."

"How? All the salespeople are either hiding or working with richer customers than I am." I throw my arm out wildly, encompassing the phantom sales clerks in my exasperation.

"You're officially a man if shopping gets you this upset. Watch and learn, my son." She squares her shoulders, tosses her hair back. "It's all about using a smile and the holiday spirit. Watch and learn."

Then my mom schools me in shopping with a woman's wiles. She marches over to the older male sales assistant, gently touches his arm and says a few words while smiling prettily. I *watch* the man leave his customer and follow her back to this counter. She explains the dilemma. He searches on the shelves under the display and produces the needed "K" pendant. Then I *learn* that another smile from Mom motivates the salesman to take an additional thirty percent off the sale price and wrap the gift in fancy paper too.

My mother is a master ninja of shopping.

"We can't stay but a few minutes. With the airports so busy this close to holidays, we've got to get there early to check in for our flight," Susan explains before she goes into the kitchen for a cup of the coffee Mom has waiting. Max and Thor are still in the bedroom.

With Cindy in rehab, Susan has surprised Kayla with a trip over Christmas break. They only stopped here at the house for a quick gift exchange.

"So, Mexico, huh?" I wrap my arms around Kayla in the pretense of warming her up from the cold outside, but really I just want to hold my girl. She doesn't object and leans in to lay her head on my shoulder, her Christmas bow jingling as she settles in.

"Yeah, Cancun. I wish you could go too." She squeezes her arms around my sides. She leans back. "We're staying at a hotel right on the beach and there's supposed to be these great open air markets and we get to go climbing on some ancient pyramids." She's talking fast with excitement and I am happy for her. We walk over and sit down together on the couch.

"Sounds great. But I want you to be careful. Don't run off with any lifeguards, or get eaten by a shark, or caught in the crossfire of rival drug lords." My voice sounds like I'm joking about this. Mostly.

"You really think I would do any of those things, mi amigo?" Kayla teases.

"Nope, but I watch the travel channel, mi amiga, so I know things."

The term *amiga* exhausts most of the left over vocabulary I learned in the sixth grade geography unit on Spain. From now on, I will have to resort to food words if I continue.

"We'll be fine." She grabs my hand. "But I will miss you."

"I'll miss you too. But we'll always have Madison, Missouri." Sometimes lines from cheesy old movies come in handy to impress your girl or make her laugh.

We both laugh when Mom yells from the kitchen. "Two minutes left until gifts!"

I stand up and grab the box with Kayla's little gift from the upper branches of the Christmas tree where I put it to keep away from Thor. He chews up the smaller presents if we don't keep an eye on him.

Kayla points to a bright red and green package with a huge bow. "You can open yours first," she says shyly. "I hope you like it. I made the bow."

I take care not to ruin the big glittery bow, but tear into the wrapping paper to find a really nice camera bag.

"Do you like it? I know you keep your camera in your dad's old bag, but this one is bigger so you'll have more room for more cameras or a tripod. I got the bag at that shop in the mall and you can exchange it, if you..." Kayla is rattling.

I kiss her. Today her lips taste like peppermint and I want to kiss her some more, but I know there's not much time before the others invade the room.

"Thank you." I grin. "And I like the bag, too."

"You're so welcome." Kayla's eyes sparkle. "So what's in that pretty little box?"

"Open it and find out." It's my turn to worry if she'll like the necklace.

Kayla unwraps the gift with shaking fingers and opens the box. "Oh, wow."

Wow is good.

She carefully pulls out the necklace from the box and turns away, so that I can put it on. For once, I'm happy Mom has Max or I help her put on her necklaces sometimes, so I know how to get the clasp fastened on the first try. The pendant rests just above Kayla's shirt and it's looks as nice as Kayla's smile. I go for another kiss when Mom announces loudly from the kitchen that it's time for gifts. I have to settle for a quick peck as Susan, Mom, and Max enter the living room followed by Thor barking out his enthusiasm for the festivities.

"Sorry kids, but we have to scoot. So, what did you get each other?" Susan asks.

Kayla and I show our mutual booty to the ladies while Max gets right down to the business of passing out the gifts. It's a holiday free-for-all with gift cards for music downloads and movie passes for Max and me, perfume and some fancy hair dryer for Mom, and some super big and colorful sunhats for Susan and Kayla to enjoy on their trip. Even Thor's remembered with a rawhide bone and a new ball for tossing.

Finally, there's just one gift left to exchange. It's for Kayla from me and I'm even more nervous whether she'll like this one. I watch her face as she opens the framed collage I have made to hang in her room from copies of photos of her and her little sister Krista. She told me one time that all of the photos were downstairs on the wall or in storage.

"Oh my goodness. Isn't this just beautiful?" Susan looks over Kayla's shoulder and reaches out a finger to caress one the letters that spell out *SISTERS*. "When you asked for those photos, I had no idea it would turn out like this."

"I know?" Mom beams proudly. "He did all of the editing on photos himself. He's so talented." It pleases me that she manages to keep from adding the phrase, *just like his dad.* I'm certain she thought about it.

"Mr. Applewhite let me use his tools and Max helped me cut, glue, and paint the boards for the frame." I'm embarrassed to take all of the credit and I'm still waiting for Kayla's response.

Kayla says nothing, just stares at the images. A tear plops down on the glass.

Oh no. I reach out to rip the frame away from her when she smiles at me.

"This means the world to me." She holds her hand out to me and I really do breathe a sigh of relief.

Thor interrupts the moment by gnawing loudly on his new bone.

Then it's flurry of expressions of gratitude and holiday wishes with hugs and kisses as Susan and Kayla head out for the airport.

Having your girlfriend gone over the holidays could be a bummer, but Mom surprises Max and me with brand new cell phones.

My first call is to Mexico. I find out later that calls out of the country aren't the free kind. Mom's reaction to the extra charges isn't at all like the *"wow"* I got from Kayla. Good thing I have a job.

"It's been three months without another death. That's good, but it don't help the ones that's already gone. Even all of those fancy agents from out of town couldn't find much to connect the little girls to each other.

It could be Peterson and Reyes girls really did just drown and some drifter killed the Cotton girl. I've got a hunch the killer's still in town, watching and waiting to find some other little girl and do it again. I hope like heck I'm wrong.

Middle of January in Missouri is cold and freezing and just miserable. But I'll take freezing weather every day of the dang year if stops this town from adding another little girl to the Floating Angels Murders body count.

Stan Boyer-Madison Patrolman

"Jamison! Quit your goofing off and get in here. I'm not paying you to be lazy and sit around on your duff."

I'm not being lazy or sitting on my duff—whatever that is—but I put down Cy's poorly scribbled notes from the January school board meeting. I've been trying to decipher enough of them to type a coherent story on the computer. I head into his office.

"You bellowed, oh reporter with the worst handwriting in history?" Normally, I don't speak to bosses or even other adults in this manner. Cy likes it. He has been teaching me the art of using sarcasm and insults as the Midwest's way for men to bond. Doesn't seem sensible to be so rude to the people you admire the most. At school, it's grounds for being disciplined for bullying. But all of the old guys down at the diner where Cy and I go down to the network over pieces of pie talk this way, and they would kill for each other.

"Didn't your parents teach you any respect for your elders?" Cy inquires.

"My dad's dead and Mom's met you, so you don't count."

"Seems like a good lovin' woman, too. Make the perfect third Mrs. Hanover to comfort me in my old age," Cy threatens.

"Told you before. Approach my mother, and we duel at dawn."

He snorts and only coughs a couple of times. The no smoking gum must be working.

"What'd you need? I'm trying to finish the school board meeting article so I can go home. I've got homework."

"For whiz kid, you sure study a lot."

"I'm a whiz kid, because I do study. Good grades equal scholarship cash. A man don't get rich working for a newspaper."

That last statement is something Cy says whenever he's trying to motivate me. He seems satisfied driving his old Cadillac, which he calls *Her Highness,* keeping a bottle of whiskey is the bottom drawer of his desk, and working at a small town newspaper. But he's always telling me how important it is for a young man like me to go out and see the world. I'd like to do that someday and I know good grades now and college are going to help get me there.

"Where's that purse thing you carry around with you?" Cy needles, changing the subject.

"I don't think you're talking about my backpack, so you must mean my camera bag."

"Yeah. The one that looks like a girl should be carrying it. Bring it in here," Cy orders.

I walk over to the door to the outer office to get it, wondering what the old guy is up to now. He's been trying to work on another story about the unsolved murders, but as far as I know, there's nothing new to photograph. Probably just wants to make more fun of my bag. We insult each other so often and so well, we are practically cultivating a Midwest Bromance at this point.

I set the bag Kayla gave me for Christmas in the middle of the desk, taking care not to disturb all of the piles of paper in his "filing" system. Cy reaches up, unfastens the center section and investigates an empty section next to the bigger one where I store Dad's old 35 mm. I usually check out a digital one from Martha at the front desk if I need to shoot something for the paper. It's smaller and easier to work with.

"That's an actual camera bag, but if you are in the mood to buy a new purse, they have 'em down at the mall." I say.

He glares over his glasses and doesn't play. "You got a lot of room in this thing, don't you?"

"Yeah, it's made for more than one camera and extra lenses."

"Guess you've got room for this then." He leans back and opens the bottom desk drawer. Could be drinking time's coming early today.

Instead Cy pulls a small camera box out. He sets it down next to my bag and I recognize the brand on the outside of the box. A nice one. Digital. Expensive.

"Why don't you try this one out and see if it fits," he suggests.

"This one's so nice, I'm surprised the paper paid for it." I already have the box in my hand and opened to study the booklet to determine the new camera's capabilities.

Cy smacks his desk happily. "Don't worry who paid for it." He says it so gruffly I realize he must have purchased the camera. "It's yours, Jamison." Then Cy may have grinned. It's so hard to tell.

"Are you kidding?" I fumble with what to say. This is such a surprise. Cy's a generous, stand-up kind of man who does a lot of nice things for people in spite of his gruff act, but this? "It's so expensive, are you sure?"

"Just say thank you, kid. Don't make this into to some sappy greeting card moment. Take it on home and figure out how to use it." Cy's voice is gruff and I don't think it's from all the years of smoking.

"I do. Thank you, I mean. This is awesome!" I start toward the door when I remember. "But I've got to finish the school board story."

"Leave it. Story will wait until tomorrow." My boss leans back in his chair and places his hands at the back of neck and smirks. "You've got homework to do, too."

I carefully put the instructions back in the box before sticking my hand out. "You're one of the good guys, Mr. Hanover. Don't ever let anyone tell you differently."

Cy looks down and then grasps my hand for a firm man-to-man handshake.

"It's Cy. I gotta get back to work." His lips remain in an artificially firm line to keep up his gruff man reputation. "Man don't get—"

"—rich working at a newspaper," I finish for him.

Maybe I'll never make a fortune as a reporter, but being able to count on a man like Cy Hanover in my corner makes me one of the wealthiest guys around.

"You and Kayla going to the Valentine's Sweetheart Dance on Saturday night?" asks Billy.

We are developing proofs in the school's dark room. Most photos are digital now, but it's in our curriculum to learn how to do it old school. Why? I don't know, because it isn't likely all of the digital cameras and printers will go down all at once.

"Yeah, we are." I lift a print with the tongs to place it in the next tray.

"What about Max? He got a date yet?"

"Nope. Says that's fine with him and he's gonna stay home and play video games.

I am a little envious of my twin. Dancing is never my favorite activity, but I'm not even sure I want to spend the evening with Kayla. After the hickey at Thanksgiving and the great gift exchange, I thought we were doing okay. Then Cindy came home from rehab and Kayla shut down again. We've exchanged a few hugs and kisses and even met for a couple of dates, but most of the time she's been tense and irritable.

"It's one of the semi-formal dances, huh? Guys wear their good pants and girls do dresses?"

"Yeah, I even ordered Kayla a corsage at Backyard Bouquets."

"Oh." Billy shoes squeak as his weight sways back and forth on his heels. "You think all girls expect one of those flower things?"

"I guess. My mom's says it's important."

"It is?" Now his voice squeaks too.

Just my luck, Billy wants dating advice.

"She also says the guy is supposed to find out the color of the girl's dress and pick out flowers and ribbon to match." I instruct while swishing the sheet around in the solution using metal tongs.

"Oh man! I have no idea what she will be wearing."

Even in the near dark I can tell Billy's preparing to have a girl-trouble induced meltdown. This is not something I want to experience with him in such a tight setting. If he cries, I'm socking him. Hard. Better to ward it off.

"It's no big deal. You can buy white and silver. Matches everything. Who're you taking?

Billy must look stricken at the question but it's too dark to tell.

"That's the problem. Nobody yet." He confessed.

"It's Tuesday." I hand him a sheet to hang up on the clothesline. "Don't you think you better ask someone?"

"What if she says no?"

"A chance every man has to take. Man up, Billy." I start on the next proof.

"Jeff's going with Claire." Billy is back to swaying back and forth and making his shoes squeak.

I hadn't heard that. At least Jeff's a pretty good guy and maybe Kayla won't act all jealous if I talk to Claire.

"I'm going to ask Jenna. She seemed to like me during football season."

"And you waited until now to make your move?" I laugh.

Billy responds loftily, "I was in training. No girls allowed during the season."

"You do know football's been done so long that basketball season is almost over, right?

"I know." He lets out a tiny sound that might be a whimper. Oh heck no. I move on quickly.

"Ask her after this in the hall. The worst she can say is no."

"Not helping, Marty."

I try another tack using a hokey fortuneteller accent. "Listen to the words of the All Knowing Marty Jamison. I have looked deep into this pool of developer and I predict you will get what you seek." Then I add. "That will be five dollars. Those who are All Knowing don't work for free."

"Dumb…" He finishes the word with a reference to an animal cousin of our school mascot, Monty the Mule. "I'll try asking her out at lunch and see what happens."

"Good luck." I think about my own upcoming date. "Girls. Can't always figure 'em out, but usually worth the effort to try."

Later that afternoon, I assume my advice paid off. Billy surprises me with such an enthusiastic high five when we pass each other in the hall that I may need to see the nurse for another icepack.

"You're okay, sweetie. Mommy's here. No, there's nobody outside your window. Craig, would you stop arguing with me for once and go outside and find out what's making that noise? It's scaring her.

It's going to be fine, your father's going to figure it all out and fix it for us. Baby, I told you there's no such thing as a real boogeyman.

Now see, Daddy says it was just a loose screen that the bad old window was blowing around. Mommy promises that nothing will get her little Victoria.

Carrie Small-Mother

21

"Hello. Where is everyone? Thor?" No answer.

It's a few days after Cy gave me the camera, and I'm home expecting to find Mom and Max already at the dinner table. I walk on through the kitchen and nearly jump out of my skin when the door to Mom's room is jerked open by Max.

"It's him." Max says to Mom who is sitting at the sewing machine behind him. He steps back and plops down on the floor next to Thor and picks up a shirt and appears to be in the middle of sewing on a button. That's different.

I step into the room carefully stepping around the huge mounds of clothes littering the floor and bed. I plop down on the bed to the sound of Mom pushing the foot on her portable sewing machine.

Thrump, Thrrrummmmpppp, Thrrrrruuummmmpppp.

"So did we open up a sweat shop while I was at work?"

"Nomm, not yyyet." Mom mumbles through a mouth full of straight pens.

I've seen her do this before and think it's strange that she's so careful with us, but willing to do this. I mean how would you explain it to the doctors if you suddenly sneeze and swallow them or shoot them like blow darts into someone.

"Mom, please let Max answer. What's going on with all of these clothes?"

Max looks up from where he is carefully tying a knot in his thread. He picks up another shirt and button.

"We're fixing all of this stuff." Maybe I should call him Mr. Obvious from now on.

"Okay. Why?"

"We have these clothes bins at the activity center where people can donate their old stuff. Mom's helping me get them ready to give away at Family Fun Day."

"Isn't it nice that Max and the janitor Mr. Coleman volunteered to do this extra project?" Thank goodness Mom has removed the pins before speaking.

"Yeah, Rudy took everything to the Laundromat and me and Mom's fixing the clothes that need it."

"Rudy?"

"Rudy is Mr. Coleman, Marty." Mom smiles. "He's the nice gentleman who's become a good friend to Max."

So Max has an older friend too. That's good. I have Cy, but I hope this Rudy didn't give Max all of the crap I got. I don't think he's ready for Hanover Handling.

"He's from Savannah, Georgia, and he's got a funny accent. Sometimes he brings me a piece of peach pie. He says he got the recipe from an old lady who lives by salt marshes."

"That's cool." My brother is getting a life without me.

"Yeah, you can meet him at Fun Day." Max reaches over and pulls out a knitted hat that he places on his head. "He found this in the clothes and gave it to me for helping out."

He looks a little goofy in it, but I nod to show I like it. It's nice to see Max so happy.

"You like the hat that much, huh? Hand me a shirt to fix."

"I like it because I'm going to wear this hat and I'm never going to comb my hair again."

"Yooouu wwwisssh." Mom mutters through a mouth full of pins.

I roll my eyes and try to thread a needle. Parents!

I move in and get a great shot of Max and his friend Rudy explaining to Madison's mayor about the free clothes program. The two of them have been beaming with pride over the service they've been able to provide the community.

I like Max's friend who turns out to be a lot shorter than I expect. I laugh when I see that the man also wears a knitted hat similar to the one he gave my brother. The man's lack of height and dorky hat don't seem to bother Max. I'm happy that today is so good for my twin, but I plan to hide out the next time the bins fill up and they want people to sew. My fingers are still sore from pricking myself trying to sew and that's been two weeks ago.

I move on to admire the baked goods that the Spanish Club from school is selling to raise funds to go to Costa Rica in the summer. That sounds like fun, but Cy's already told me to plan on working for him. In fact, I'm working today for the paper, taking photos.

"Hi Marty, thinking about getting some sopapillas?" Claire slides in front of the stand beside me.

"Who isn't? They smell so good."

"I agree. I've been over passing out safety information with StuCo and I just couldn't wait anymore. Wanna share?" Claire looks up at me hopefully.

Man, I hate to say no, but Kayla's here too. Her dance team is selling crafts to fundraise for new pompons. I take a quick glance around and don't see her, but I know she will not like me sharing dessert with another girl. Claire especially.

"Uh, I better not. I'm watching my, uh, weight." I pat my non-existent belly.

"Okay." Claire's face falls. "That's okay. Everybody puts on excess weight during the winter."

I jump when two arms suddenly encircle my waist before fingers are locked into my front belt loops. Kayla.

"I guess you would know all about that, wouldn't you, Claire? Excess weight, I mean."

Well, that was mean. Claire's not as thin as Kayla, but her curves work for her.

"I'll see you later, Marty!" Claire spins on the heels of her tall black boots and goes quickly clicking away.

I disengage Kayla's hands from my belt loops and set her to the side. "Do you have to treat her that way? She wasn't doing anything."

"Whatever. You know she likes you. I'm not going to stand by and watch her try to steal you away from me."

"She can't steal me if I want to be with you."

"If?" Her blue eyes blaze.

I don't know the proper adjective for brown eyes that show anger, but whatever it is, I am sure that's what mine look like right now.

"That's what you got out of what I said? You didn't hear the part about wanting to be with you!" My voice is loud enough that a few of the parents and kids look over.

I grab Kayla's hand and lead her outside away from the crowds. It doesn't take long to realize it's still too cold from the snow covering the ground to stay long. Neither of us speak at first. Then Kayla breaks the silence.

"You're right. That was unfair of me. You're one of the few people I've been able to count on." Kayla is rubbing her arms through the long-sleeved spandex dance suit she and the other girls wear today.

She can count on me. I'm a loyal boyfriend. Still, I recognize that the potential is there for something to develop between me and Claire if I wasn't with Kayla. Maybe she's got a right to be possessive.

"I'm sorry." My guilt has me reaching forward and she comes into my arms. "I didn't mean to yell at you."

"It's okay. I upset you." Kayla leans back. "We're still going to the Valentine's Dance together next weekend, right?" She shivers.

I'm actually still kind of upset with her, but it's too cold out here to continue this argument.

"Sure." I turn and head back inside without looking to see if she follows me this time.

All right KMON listeners, we got a mini spring thaw coming up this week. The weather center up at Happy Hills says we'll be warming up to the mid-40's by Tuesday and by Thursday afternoon all this white stuff will just be a memory. I'll tell you right now, first thing Friday morning, I'm going to take my car up to Otto's Car Wash and clean all the salt and mud off. Give me a call and tell me what you've got planned for all of the warm weather at...

Bucky T. Dodd-KMON Radio Deejay

22

"Hold still!" Mom tugs at my neck. She's either trying to straighten the knot in my tie or choke me to death. I'm not sure which one I prefer. I hate dressing up.

"Can't I just pretend I am a rapper and wear a sports jersey?"

I already know this plea will be denied by the woman who has years of experience corralling Max and me for unwanted grooming. So far she hasn't put spit on her finger to wipe a spot off my face. She still may.

"No, you cannot. There!" Mom steps back and looks me over. She turns me to face the hall mirror. "Now you look like the handsome gentleman I've raised you to be."

I look and it's better than usual. My dark eyes and hair look good with the long-sleeved black shirt and dress pants. Mom's made certain my socks, belt, and shoes are black too. The only color is a red tie that we bought to match Kayla's dress.

I still protest for the principle. "I would rather be a member of the Mafia. In their TV shows they get to wear un-tucked bowling shirts with their dress pants." I complain loudly and try to loosen my collar.

"And all those men in their bowling shirts all end up dead in a dumpster in New Jersey, too." I forgot. Mom watches those shows too. "Now Martin Joseph, don't mess up that tie! Do you have Kayla's corsage and the candy box?"

In addition to the expected corsage, I'm giving Kayla her Valentine's Day gift tonight. My mom knows someone from the hospital who makes fancy heart-shaped wooden shadow boxes. I bought one and Mom helped me fill it with a bunch of girl stuff like lip-gloss, perfumes, and hair things, as well as some fancy little individually wrapped chocolates.

"Yeah Mom, I've got it under control. You're the one getting all excited," I tease.

"Well, it's your first real dance with a date." Mom takes a breath. "You didn't set that candy down where Thor could reach it, did you? Remember Halloween that year?"

"Of course. That's when we all learned dogs are allergic to chocolate. The vet said it's a wonder that finishing off my candy didn't kill him. He was one *sick puppy*!" I throw out the last line to motivate Mom to lighten up a little.

"Martin Joseph! That is not funny."

Mom's right. It was a bad pun and in really poor taste, since Thor had been really sick.

"The corsage and present are on the counter by the utility porch. I'll get them on my way out. I told you I've got everything under control."

"If you say so. Let me write Max a note. I wish he would have gone stag or asked a girl to this dance. Your brother hasn't been his usual self since Jacob's arrest, and he and his mom moved to St. Louis. Hopefully that boy has given up the tagging and vandalism."

Mentioning Jacob reminds me that Max's never told Mom about tagging, so I change the subject. "Max's been working late at the center a lot these days."

"Yes, and he never answers his cell phone when I try to call him there. I don't know why I bought him a cell phone if he never uses it."

"Maybe he doesn't have good service there. So, would you like for me to back the car out of the garage? You know, since you might be tired from work and all," I offer.

Mom laughs at my blatant tactic to get more driving time.

"Okay. You can drive. "

I take the keys from the hanger by the door and pull on Dad's old leather jacket. I'm not thrilled about wearing it, but Mom insisted Dad's jacket will be perfect for the warmer weather we are having uncharacteristically in February. Another example of Missouri's crazy weather, snowy and freezing last week and warm and muddy this one.

I would have been happy with my old purple hoodie, if Kayla still didn't have it. I like that she wears it most of the time.

Being trusted to back Mom's car out of the garage without her in it supervising makes me feel better about the night. She's been really good about taking Max and I out to drive the car more often, now that our sixteenth birthdays are coming up. Mom's car isn't cool, but it's going to be the only one available until Max and I come up with enough money for a car we can share. Then we have to pay to insure both of us. To save money, I suggested we could just pretend to be the same driver and fool the cops. Mom voted no.

Once in the car, I run through all of the checkpoints for driving before successfully backing up. I told Mom that I have everything under control! Then she comes out of the house with her purse and waves Kayla's corsage and the shadow box I left on the counter.

Maybe the *everything* part is a slight exaggeration.

"I'm sorry Marty. I can't imagine why Kayla is so late. Let me try her cell phone again." Cindy goes into the kitchen to get her phone. It's good to see her acting more like regular mom since she came home to stay last month. I do wish it wasn't due to worrying about Kayla's whereabouts.

I remain on the living room sofa where I've been waiting for forty minutes for Kayla to show up. We've already missed our ride to dinner. Billy has his license, so he and Jenna were going to pick us up here in time to go to dinner before the dance. Kayla's running so late they finally went on without us. Cindy will have to give us a ride, if Kayla ever shows up.

I hope that she didn't change her mind. Things have been a little cool between us since our argument at the activity center. I have hopes that tonight will clear up anything negative between us, but she needs to show up first.

"No answer." Cindy chews her lip as she returns. "Let me run over to Susan's before she leaves for her date with the attorney. Maybe Kayla's contacted her." She hurries through the connecting door of the duplexes.

I take my cell out and try again. Straight to voicemail. No response to my texts either. I look out the front windows and it's nearly dark. I stand to pace.

I'm worried. There's a possible serial killer running around town, after all. I know Kayla doesn't fit the killer's usual type of victim based on her age, but there's always some weird person out there just waiting to throw girls in the back of their van.

Why is it always a *van?* Don't killers ever drive a compact or jeep or one of those square foreign cars that look like toasters?

I stop pacing and fan my underarms to prevent further sweating in my dress shirt. I had hopes of getting to the actual dance before becoming a perspiring beast. Dad's coat might be good for the cooler weather outside, but I really don't want to wear it inside the gym to cover sweat stains.

I move over to the sofa to study the family photos hanging behind it. The first photo of Kayla's parents wedding proves she got her hair color and her smile from her mom and her chin from her dad. It surprises me that Cindy keeps this one up. She's open about her anger toward him taking off after their youngest daughter died. I know Kayla's got some life insurance money set aside in a trust from his death benefits, but she doesn't talk much about him.

I look over to the other portrait. Kayla is around five or six and Krista's a chubby two-year-old blond mini-me nestled in her lap. Their dresses are bright blue like their eyes and they both have huge matching hair bows on their ponytails, like the kind Kayla does in her craft class at the center.

There's one more thing I realize about my girlfriend as I study this photo. I've never seen her smile as broadly as she is in this picture with her sister. Kayla must really miss Krista. It makes me realize that even though Max gets on my nerves, my life would be different if he were suddenly gone.

The front door bursts open and Kayla isn't smiling as she throws off my muddy purple hoodie and kicks off her equally muddy shoes. Her hair is wild around her face and her breaths rush in and out quickly. I feel a little guilty at how hard she must have been hurrying. I take a step toward her and she starts, realizing I am here.

"I am so sorry that I'm late, Marty. First a little girl spilled a bunch of paint on the craft table and I had to...clean it up." She runs her fingers through her hair trying to smooth it down. Kayla glances down at the mud on her clothes and shoes and then adds, "I had to stop on the way and help someone out..." Kayla sucks in a deep breath. "...of the ditch. I got muddy."

"It's okay. But we missed our ride to dinner." I stop just short of hugging her. I mean, I am dressed up and she's pretty messy. Then she sniffles.

To heck with looking good. I cross the rest of the distance to hug my girl when Cindy rushes into the room and fires off a barrage of comments and questions.

"There you are! Where have you been? Marty and I were worried to death. You're a mess. What happened?"

She doesn't even pause for answers, just pushes Kayla toward the stairs up to the bedrooms. "Sit down, Marty. I'll have her ready to go in ten minutes. We can go to a drive-thru on the way, so you two won't starve."

I sat down as directed and listen to the muted sounds of the shower start and stop, quiet talking, mini crashes, the roar of a blow dryer and finally several hisses of hairspray. It's actually twenty minutes before they return and all I can think when Kayla comes downstairs is how tonight's wait has been worth every minute.

"You're beautiful." I blurt out before blushing.

"No, I'm not." Kayla blushes too as she smoothes down her shiny blond hair.

She's done something to it that makes it super straight and shiny. I like that the short red dress makes her legs look especially long. Her eyes sparkle and I can't wait to kiss off tonight's sparkly lip-gloss and determine its flavor. Cindy enters the room with her coat before I can try.

"Don't you two look so wonderful?" Her voice cracks, but she quickly recovers. "Marty, why don't you help Kayla with her corsage while I grab my camera for a quick picture?"

Kayla smells much better than the corsage and my hand shakes while I try to figure out how to pin it on. She giggles at my attempt to keep from poking either of us with the pin, or touching her chest in front of her mom once she returns. A couple of quick photos of us standing together in front of the sofa and then I help Kayla into her dress coat. After a quick meal of fast food in the car with Cindy, my girl and I arrive at the dance. I hate mushy stuff, but I have the best night of my life. I think that Kayla has her best night, too.

And why wouldn't it be? Our friends are there. The deejay plays music we both like with plenty of slow dances for me to hold Kayla close. The principal only taps me on the shoulder once to remind me to put more space between our bodies. He isn't looking at all when Kayla and I make out over by the end of the bleachers. On the way home Billy doesn't kill us with his driving on our way to have dessert at the local Open All Nite Diner, or when we all are dropped off one by one at our homes.

Getting ready for bed that night, I still smile like an idiot as I undress in the dark. Max is out for the count tonight over on his side of the room and snoring like he's been there for a while. It would have been nice if Max had asked a girl to come to the dance and gone too, but I'm kind of glad he didn't.

Sometimes a person doesn't want to share every experience with his brother. Even one who is a lot like him.

I've been an EMT for sixteen years here in Madison. I got my training as a Corpsman in the Army. I saw some action back when I served.

I went out on the calls for the Peterson and Cotton girls. But this thing with someone drowning those little girls... I didn't have to deal with anything as tragic when I was overseas. Sure, I had guys die on me. And I treated some young guys too, but they were still men. They knew what to expect comin' in. But those little girls were too young to know much of anything.

And then it happened again.

Matt Clark-Madison EMT

23

Jamison, get in here!"

I jump. This isn't Cy's usual bellow. Something's wrong.

I fly up out of the chair where I've been putting a story together on local crop predictions for the coming growing seasons. Normally on a Saturday I don't work, but Cy's been busy doing a special investigative piece rehashing the facts of Floating Angels Murders. He had me come in to do some of the more boring stuff. Whatever has Cy so excited doesn't sound boring.

"Grab that fancy camera of yours and a jacket." Cy's out of his own chair frantically searching through the papers on his desktop. "Where are they?" He rips open his center drawer.

"What are you looking for? What's going on?"

Cy doesn't even pause in his searching. "Car keys! We've got a story. Guy found another little girl."

Horrible news.

But a chance to work on a real news story? At a real crime scene? Heck yeah!

I dive into the piles of paper closest to me. "Check your whiskey drawer."

"How do you know about that?" He reaches for the handle.

"Everyone who works here knows about it. Are they there?"

"Yes. Go! If we hurry we'll be the first press there." He rounds his desk at a run. Still, I have my camera bag, coat, and am already waiting at the car when Cy gets to it.

He may have the years of experience of a reporter going to a crime scene, but I have the speed and agility of a motivated teenager.

"Watch that pothole! You said you knew how to drive." Cy yells while maintaining his death grip on the dash of his car. "We'll lose the exhaust that way."

"I can drive. I am driving. You can't even see where we're going, so how do you know where the potholes are anyway?"

Cy managed to find the car keys, but left his glasses somewhere on the mess of his desk. He really doesn't see well enough to drive without them, so he threw the keys to me and ordered me to drive. I was too excited to reveal I don't have a real license yet. Now we're on our way to the old quarry that sits just barely inside Madison's legal boundaries. It's so old the actual road hasn't been paved for years and is little more than a rough path.

"Memory. I used to go bird hunting using this road in the fall. Keep your eyes up ahead. "

"Maybe if this thing was a truck or something more than three inches off the ground…" Loud crash as we hit another deep rut on the way up to the quarry, "I wouldn't hit every single piece of gravel or mud hole we drive over." Another crash.

"Jamison, when this day is over, I'm going to kick your tookus for treating Her Highness like this," Cy threatens.

He probably isn't serious. Although, this big old beast of a car is one of Cy's pride-and-joys. Huge, made of real metal, and worthy of a crown, which is why he refers to it as Her Highness. He yells again as we take another hard thump making the front and back of the car bounce up and down.

It's not a good time to admit to Cy that he has put his precious car baby into the hands of a lawbreaker. Fortunately, this road back into the quarry is deserted and there's a big field at the side to pull into if I really mess up driving.

"Listen up, when we get there, you just stay back and let me talk. These officials won't let us get close enough to the actual crime scene for you to take pictures of anything good. You try to sneak in some background stuff we can use for the front page before they shut us down."

I'm not even sure how Cy knows when stuff like this happens. I asked him once. He told me the old saying about newspapermen and the confidentiality of source is still true in his book. Never give up your sources and be willing to go to jail protecting them. I believe Cyrus Hanover is the kind of man who would.

Hopefully neither of us is going to jail today for any crime, because we have gotten as close as we can.

At the old rusted gate that is now open and leads directly into the old quarry, two Madison police cars are parked next to an old farm truck. I see only one person. A police officer stands on the service road to block further access. He does not look happy to see us. At all.

I steer the car onto the edge of the field to park and sit up as tall as I can, trying to make it appear that I am a legal driver. Multiple sirens getting closer to our location mean we only have a short time before the scene is overrun with other press. Another girl's death is big news.

It's sad reality, but arriving at the scene before other news media is our little paper's chance to get a scoop.

Cy doesn't even wait for the car to completely stop, much less be shoved into park, before he jumps out and hurries toward the officer.

I busy myself getting my smaller camera out of the bag. I know the area at the bottom of the big hill leading up here, because most of the town kids have crawled through the barbed wire fences to cut across on our way to other parts of town. Max uses it to get back and forth from the activity center when it's not covered in snow or too muddy.

I look up toward where the actual quarry is located. From this vantage point there isn't much to see except the faded posted warning sign on the gate, dead grass, and some scraggily trees. Good.

I'm not sure I am enough of a hardened reporter to see a body. Especially if there really is a dead little girl beyond the trees. I shiver, more from being creeped out than from being cold in the gray hoodie Mom bought me to replace the one Kayla kept after the fair.

I look around and understand the site's popularity with the party crowd. It's close to everything, yet higher up and out of view, so from a killer's perspective it's the perfect location to commit a crime. That I know this creeps me out even more. I snap a couple of shots of the sign on the gate and one down toward town. I turn back and try to listen to what the officer is saying. It's not welcoming.

"Cy, you know you can't go up there. It's a secure scene." The officer's face is ashen and he looks more than a little upset and not the mad kind.

"Don't worry, Stan. The kid and I will stay back. We're not like those pushy big city reporters. But the kid, here, might want to take a couple of pictures later if you can get us closer to the action."

I do? Maybe of the crime scene. Much later after the body is removed. I'm not ready to photograph shots of bodies. At least, not dead bodies. I haven't progressed to taking racy photos of live bodies. I barely even take selfies with my phone.

The officer's quite blunt with a refusal to the possibility of photos at any point. Relief! I listen as Cy tries to cajole the officer into giving up some information.

"Just give me something. Is it another drowning?"

The officer glares straight ahead and makes no comment.

"I already know Floyd Olsen said he found a little girl when he came up here to cut some firewood."

Officer Stan's face flushes and he slaps the side of his leg with his hand. "Cy, I swear someone is going to lose their job if the chief ever finds out who leaks all of this information to you," he complains.

"Now, Stan. Let me help. Our town's already got three little girls dead and nobody to pay for it. Now, a possible fourth. If I go back right now and get the information out to the other papers, maybe we can catch this killer," Cy offers evenly.

The loud, shrill whine lets us know that the ambulance has topped the rise. It's moving slowly and the driver appears to be having as much trouble navigating the ambulance through the ruts in the road as I did with Her Highness. We all start when the driver turns the siren off. Guess the sight of us standing there inactive is enough for the driver to know there's nothing much to be done to help anyone at the top of the hill.

"It's too many dead, Stan. It has to stop. I can get the word out. Help find somebody who knows something." Cy voice is soft, yet reverberates in the still air.

Stan walks closer to the edge of the road to wave the ambulance on up to the scene. He doesn't even turn his head when he chokes out, "This one didn't drown. She went over the side and hit the rocks before she reached water. Sometime yesterday is my guess."

He strides past us.

"Someone help her hit those rocks, Stan?" Cy tries one more time to get the information he wants.

The officer has no answer as the ambulance travels past us up the hill, then he looks straight at Cy and nods a silent affirmation.

Cy motions me back to the car. We have gotten all the news we are going to find out today. I've got pictures to get ready and Cy's got a story to write to help catch a serial killer.

With another little girl dead, it doesn't seem too important to mention that I'm still driving illegally.

Why did you try to run from me?

You made me chase you and then you fell. Now all I can hear is your scream and the sounds of you bouncing off those rocks and then nothing.

If you had waited, I would have made this so much easier for you.

The Killer

24

It's almost six when I enter the back porch. I hang my camera bag up on a hook in the entry way, kick off my shoes, and throw them next to Max's muddy ones in the wicker basket Mom keeps on the utility porch. It's her method for us to keep from tracking up the floor. Sometimes it even works.

It's been a long day. Once we returned to the newspaper office, I prepared and cropped the photos and helped check facts. Cy worked in his office reviewing his notes and contacting experts for more information and quotes. His theory is this latest girl is another victim of the serial killer targeting girls here in Madison. He's still at the office, but the newspaper's bookkeeper, Martha, volunteered to bring me home. Nobody's in favor of me walking home in the dark with a killer on the loose. I could've refused the ride and been insulted that my coworkers didn't think I can take care of myself, but today's been an odd combination of morbidly exciting, and emotionally and physically tiring. I was grateful for the lift.

After today I've decided it might be better to stick to writing about the boring stuff like school board meetings and farm report summaries. Much less sadness.

On the drive, Martha and I try to guess the identity of this last little girl. We come up with nothing to explain why nobody's noticed she's been gone at least since yesterday. We also wonder what kind of person would "help" her onto those rocks and if it was the same person who's been drowning those other girls.

Walking in the kitchen, I hear someone just getting out of the shower. Mom, most likely. She'd called the paper earlier to check on me. I cross to the sink and turn up the faucet handle to gulp greedily at the cool water. Then I splash my face and grab a couple of paper towels to dry it.

I really don't feel so great. Working on a story like this one makes you start to wonder about bad things. What if the little girl didn't die right away after hitting those rocks? Did she cry out for help? For her mom or her dad? And the worst one…how could anyone just leave her there all alone?

I swallow hard. I'm not the only person unsettled by all of these possibilities tonight. I fully expect Cy to take a drink or two from the bottle in his bottom drawer, and not the celebration kind.

I ball up the paper towels and shoot them haphazardly toward the trash can when a still dripping Mom comes barreling in the kitchen in her sweats, dog slippers, and an old shirt of Dad's. She doesn't say a word, just gives me a rib-crushing hug.

It's been such a crummy day that I hug her back for a full thirty seconds. This is becoming a habit around here.

"Are you sure you are okay? What was Cy thinking, taking you up there?" she demands.

"I told you when you called, I'm fine, Mom. I didn't do anything except take a couple of pictures. The police had the area shut off when we got there."

"Well, thank goodness. I have worried all afternoon about you."

"Mom." Some of exhaustion and irritation at my perception of being treated like a baby comes through in my tone of voice.

Mom takes a big breath. "I'm sorry. There's just been so many deaths."

I change the subject. "Where's Max?"

"Oh, that was another problem. Right now, he's asleep." She crosses to the table and sits down wearily. "I know you were at the dance late last night, but Max had a rough one while you were gone. When I got home last night he was covered in mud and really upset. He lost his cell phone on the way home from the activity center. I finally got him to calm down and get cleaned up before I gave him a sleeping pill."

"I wondered why he snored louder than normal." I sat down next to her.

"He gets that snoring from your father, Michael. He was so loud that I used to sneak out and sleep on the couch. I had to get my rest, because you boys got up early. He always complained that he missed me." Mom smiles at her memory. At least not all of hers are bad where Dad is concerned. "I haven't even had a chance to ask you about the dance? Did you and Kayla have a good time?

"Yes, we had a great time."

After today, the events of yesterday seem like a long time ago.

Thor wanders into the kitchen and I bend down to scratch his neck.

"So did Max sleep all day?"

It doesn't seem likely, but the pills do knock him out.

"No, he was up this afternoon and ate some lunch. You know how he is when he gets himself all riled up." She closes the textbook on the table she had been studying from before I got home.

"So it was his phone that got him that upset?"

"That's what he told me."

I hope it's the truth and my brother wasn't doing something like more tagging. It's true that when Max gets really upset, he fixates and then stresses to the point it can throw his chemical balance off. It's an unpleasant way his bipolar can manifest. When we were kids, I usually could calm Max down, maybe by doing the robot story, sometimes just by talking to him. Since I had been at the dance with Kayla last night, Mom resorted to a sleeping pill. Those tend to take a while to get out of his system.

"He said he dropped it somewhere on his way home from the center. Looked all over for it until it was dark and got himself covered with mud."

"Thank you, Marty. I think he got so upset because he worries I can't come up with the money to replace the phone." Mom confides. "You know how he never wants to cause problems for anyone."

I understand why Max doesn't want to bother Mom. While other parents might lecture my twin for being irresponsible, ours realizes that sometimes bad things happen beyond the control of good people. She lived through it with Dad.

"It's just a phone." I sit up. "I'll go out with him tomorrow and look for it."

"That would be good. Speaking of doing good things? I figured with a day like today, you would appreciate your favorites. Mushroom steak and homemade mashed potatoes for dinner."

"I thought I smelled heaven."

"Just let me finish everything up. Why don't you go on in and watch some television or something in the living room? Maybe stay out of your bedroom, so Max can sleep until the food is ready."

I really would rather crawl in my own bed and cover my head with my pillow and make this day go away, but I get up to do as Mom asks while she begins pulling food out of the oven and refrigerator.

"Oh, and Kayla called earlier. She wants you to call her back."

In the living room, I plop down on the couch. Thor follows me and jumps up beside me, covering the remote. Once I roll him off of it, I turn to one of the channels that will have the late news show starting soon. I want to hear what they are reporting. Bet they don't have everything Cy and I got. I hit mute and dig my phone out of the pocket of my jeans to call Kayla. I'd finally had to turn it off at the office, because I was getting so many calls and texts coming in. Phone starts dinging as soon as I power it up. I'll look at all of them later. I push Kayla's number.

"Hello."

"Hi, it's me. Marty." This is dumb. She has caller I.D. and already knows it's me, but I'm too tired to care.

"Are you okay? I've been calling and texting your cell all day. Your mom said you were working at the paper. Did you have to go up to that quarry…" Kayla voice shakes, "where they found the little girl?"

"Yeah, I went. Sorry about the phone. Cy had me so busy at the newspaper office I didn't even have time to look at it." I pause before adding, "You're such a good girl for worrying about me."

Could I say anything goofier? I really must be tired.

Kayla doesn't even seem to notice.

"Is it true? Did another little girl drown up there?" Kayla's voice cracks a little at the end. Every little girl who dies must remind her of her sister.

It's a sad fact that when you've lost someone close to you that each new death can throw you right back into the gut-wrenching pain of the ones that came before. Today I've thought about my dad more than I want to admit to anyone.

"Well, I didn't really get too close to find out much. I don't think the police know a whole lot. When I left work, the girl's name hadn't been released yet."

Kayla lets out a long whimpering breath.

Oh man, I can't take this. I try to think of something else to talk about.

"Marty, I think you're so brave for going up there. I don't think I could do it."

192

Kayla's words make me think I really have accomplished something, so I decide to share a little insider information with her. It'll all be in the paper by morning anyways.

"Keep this quiet, but this one didn't drown. She fell."

It's a moment before Kayla says anything. "That's so horrible."

She's right. It is horrible. I've been keeping my eyes open, so I don't picture that little girl plummeting toward the rocks.

I hear Kayla gulp. "How do you know that? Did the police tell you?"

"I just know."

"Oh, I thought it might have been some kind of an accident? You know, like maybe she got lost and tripped and hit the rocks by herself? Did anyone say anything like that?"

Crud. As comforting as it might be to confirm that this was an accident instead of the result of the serial killer, I can't get away with that half-truth even to make Kayla feel better. Trying to decide what to say to her, I look up and notice the news is on now and the murder is the lead story.

"Not exactly. Hold on, Kayla. I want to hear what the reporter on television is saying about what happened." I set the phone down and grab the remote and turn it up as Thor jumps off the couch. I am relieved to see that the reporter doesn't look like she got any closer to the crime scene than Cy and I did.

"…saying that another young life has been lost here at the former Myers and Sons Quarry, located in the small town of Madison, MO. Madison, as you will recall from my earlier investigative reports, is home to what we here at Channel Six call the Floating Angels Murders. Police have yet to confirm the identity or age of the deceased. However, speculation among local community members is this latest victim is probably another young female, possibly drowned in a deep lake left by strip mining here at the quarry. Again, all we know…"

Cy's going to get his scoop that the girl fell to her death if the police don't announce what's happened before the special morning issue of the paper comes out.

" …is that someone has died at the quarry."

I mute the television to finish talking with Kayla when I notice Max is standing in the doorway of the living room staring at the television screen. He staggers a few steps into the room with Thor waiting close by, probably for Max to pet him. Our pet might hang out with me when my twin isn't around, but our whole family knows who is this dog's best friend.

"Kayla, did you …" I never finish my question, because Thor suddenly growls and then yelps in pain as the sound of a loud crash rolls across the living room.

The dog's best friend just passed out on top of him.

My husband and I are so blessed to have the Jamison family for neighbors. The ones on the other side of us barely acknowledge us, but Mary Jo and her boys are always willing to help out. We hire the twins to mow, trim the lawn, and shovel snow for us. Very responsible and polite young men.

Of course we couldn't tell which one was which for several years. Marty, the oldest, is just as smart as a whip. And Max, well, that boy is so good with animals. He dotes on that dog of his. Always taking him for a walk. Stays outside most evenings and plays catch with it.

Salt of the earth, that family is. Such good people.

Mrs. Thelma Applewhite

25

"How's Max doing?"

It's the Monday after Max passed out and I'm glad Kayla asks. I close my locker and put my arm around her waist to walk to our next classes. For me, it's environmental science and for Kayla, her dreaded P.E. class.

"Better. He's here at school today. Mom talked to his regular doctor at the hospital yesterday before they released him in the evening. He says Max's med levels got off from the combo of his regular meds and sleeping pills, so they're doing more blood tests after school today before Mom takes him to shop for a new phone."

I went out yesterday afternoon to search for Max's phone near the activity center. I saw a lot of official looking vehicles involved in the investigation along the way, but no phone. It's so muddy out there Mom figures it's ruined and a lost cause.

I'm relieved that Max didn't become a lost cause too, so I squeeze Kayla with a little hug.

"I thought your mom might keep him home. Or you might." She smiles.

Our mutual protectiveness where Max is concerned is no secret to anyone, but Kayla was still on the phone the other evening when all heck broke out. She knows how freaked out I was when I saw Max down on the floor. She actually heard me screaming to Mom for help and trying to hush Thor from barking at Max. We think he was trying to help Max up, but I finally had to put the dog in the bathroom and shut the door. My panicked yelling ended about by the time Max became conscious and the EMT's pronounced he would be okay. Ironically, landing on Thor is what saved Max from the possibility of a severe head injury. Good dog.

I was really relieved Kayla hadn't been able to see me when I almost passed out after the EMTs loaded Max up on the stretcher. I had to sit down with my head between my knees for a few minutes after I saw how much my brother on the stretcher resembled our dad in his coffin.

"Mom wanted to keep him home, but some veterinarian's bringing animals with him to talk about his career today in one of Max's classes. He didn't want to miss it."

"Learning about being a vet might be a good idea if Max is going around falling on your dog." She giggles.

Kayla wouldn't be joking if she didn't already know that Thor hadn't been hurt. Mom even rewarded him with some of the steak and mushroom gravy for taking one for the team.

I smile another goofy smile at Kayla and bend down to sneak a kiss.

"Miss Gallagher, are you so weak in your core area that you need your young man to hold you up? Perhaps I could increase the intensity of your workouts with additional abdominal crunches to better enable you to stand upright unassisted?"

Busted by Coach Fritz, P.E. Nazi.

"No thank you, Coach. Bye, Marty!" Kayla breaks away and sprints toward the locker room. I duck my head and hurry off in the opposite direction from Coach to make my own quick escape.

I like my abs just the way they are.

Mr. Collins expounds on the dangers of plastic bags to streams and wildlife when a guy named Shawn bursts into class, holding a pink discipline pass from the office. I don't know him all that much, even though we worked on a group project in this class earlier in the year. However, everyone in my grade knows of his history of getting sent to the office frequently. He drops the pass off on the teacher's desk and plops down into his assigned seat near the front of the room. As soon as the teacher turns back the board, Shawn flips in his seat and appears to be silently and emphatically mouthing a message. To me. What the heck?

Proving teachers really do have eyes in the back of their heads, Mr. Collins states, "Face the front, Shawn."

He complies, but reaches into his hoodie pocket and holds up his phone for a second before putting his hand back in his pocket. That's the sign that he's going to text someone. Our school allows students to have cell phones, but anyone caught using them in class is disciplined. I know he probably still has my phone number because of the project, and Shawn has proven his willingness to walk on the wild side.

I reach in my own hoodie pocket just as I feel the tell tale vibration. It's my turn to walk on the wild side. I slide my phone out, unlock it, and read, *"Bro w/ cops in ofis."*

What? I look up to see Shawn nodding back emphatically over his shoulder.

"Shawn!"

He turns toward the front again, having delivered his message.

Why is Max with the police? Okay, don't panic. Maybe someone found his phone and turned it in to the police and they're returning it. That doesn't sound right. They would just call or bring it by the house. Wait, what if Jacob got in trouble out in St. Louis and in exchange for immunity ratted Max out for the tagging? No, that's too much like a movie. Oh man, I've got to know what's going on.

"Mr. Collins, I gotta hurl!" I jump up and burst out into the hall.

It doesn't even feel like a lie when I get close enough to the office to witness two officers escorting Max out the front door. I take off running.

"Martin, as uh, I told you, my uh, hands are tied. I can't let you uh, leave school during the regular school day uh, unless your mother or uh, someone on your uh, emergency card 'OK's it." Principal Morris of stuttering fame searches my face to see if he's getting anywhere.

He isn't. I don't care one bit about what he was says now or earlier during his lecture concerning the consequences I could have faced for trying to follow Max and the police out the front door.

I guess I was lucky that my history teacher and the wrestling coach saw me coming down the hall and guessed where I was heading. They both grabbed me and kept me pinned against the wall cussing and yelling at them until the patrol car left. I should have punched someone, so I could get arrested and be with Max. At least I would know why they took him in. For now, I continue to cross my arms and glare at my captor.

Principal Morris sighs, "I uh, understand you are uh, upset about your uh, uh, brother."

I say nothing, because nothing is going to satisfy me but leaving to find Max. It's already been about three or four hours, and Mom hasn't answered any of the calls from the school or me. I'm sure she's at the station with Max. Susan's on my school emergency contact card too, but there's no response from her either when I call. That leaves the third name on the list and I've left him a message, but he's not here yet. Probably had a doctor's appointment, but I have faith he will be here soon.

The principal's intercom buzzes.

"Principal Morris, there is a Mr. Applewhite out here to pick up Marty Jamison."

Bingo! My savior arrives.

I don't even pause for Principal Morris to stutter out a goodbye.

"Thank you, Mr. Applewhite. Yes, I'll call and let you know when I find out what is happening. Goodbye."

I shut the door of the small car and trot into the police station. I'm grateful for my neighbor picking me up and bringing me to the station, but he's in his eighties and drives well below the speed limit. I'm so anxious to find out what is happening with Max that I'd considered jumping out a couple of miles back and running the rest of the way.

At the reception desk, a woman stares at her computer screen. After waiting for what seems like a whole minute for her to look up and acknowledge me, but is really only a few seconds, I lean in and say loudly, "I need to find Maxwell Jamison. He was picked up earlier today from the high school." I can't help the bitter tone that slips out in my last statement.

She must be used to people using that tone, because she still stares at her computer screen. "How old is your brother?"

"Fifteen. Almost sixteen. Like me. We're twins." I don't why I feel the need to add that last information. Nerves, maybe. I've never been to the police station.

"Then you need the juvenile division. Take that elevator down to the first floor and sign in at their desk. They can help you."

I stride over to the elevator doors and punch the button. Now that I know I am close to finding Max, I want to hurry even more. When it arrives, I jump in and choose the appropriate level. I study my reflection in the shiny walls surrounding me. Man, I look stressed and I can't even imagine what Max must look like by now. Not good, I'll bet.

Ding. The doors open and I step out.

Two patrolmen are in the hall. They stare intently at me.

"What are you doing out here?" the first demands, squaring his shoulders.

"Why isn't someone with you?" asks the other stepping closer.

These officers look at me like I'm doing something wrong.

"Me? I'm looking for…" I don't finish before I'm flanked on either side by these big men with guns.

"Come with us."

I'm totally mystified by their reactions to me until I glimpse the reflections of our little parade in the glass as we walk by one of the pictures on the wall. Then I grin. They think I'm Max. I can explain that I'm not, but I have the feeling they are escorting me straight to my objective. My brother.

"O.M.G.! Carson told me he was by the office and saw the police haul Max Jamison away in a squad car. It must be serious, because his brother Marty came running up and lost it. Teachers had to hold him down. Then Carson overheard the secretary say something about the Floating Angels Murders.

I hope Max isn't the killer. Both Jamison boys are kind of cute. I love tall guys with dark hair and chocolate brown eyes. But Max is the one that's kind of weird, right?

Hey Blake and Carlee, did you hear that Max Jamison is the one doing the Floating Angels Murders? Carson was in the office when the police arrested him.

Erica Goodwin-MHS Sophomore

26

"Where's Max?" I demand as I jump out of my seat when Mom comes into the precinct's lobby, where Kayla, Susan, and her lawyer boyfriend, Nathan Landry, wait. It feels like we've been there for days, but it's only been a couple of hours. Kayla's here now, too. Cindy dropped her off before she went to her AA meeting.

All we've been able to find out so far is that Max is being interviewed about his whereabouts on Friday night.

"He's still inside."

"You left him alone with the cops? Mom!" I clench my fists as I picture Max in the dark being beaten by burly patrolmen. Proof I watch too many cop shows.

"Calm down. The juvenile advocate is in there with him. It's his job to protect Max." Mom runs her hand through her hair and I recognize this self-comforting habit she did a lot after Dad killed himself. "Right now he's having a soda. I came out because the detectives said you all were out here and I wanted to give you an update."

Mom's pretty calm, but her face is pale in spite of her bright pink scrubs she's wearing from work. I'm not the only one concerned about my mom, because Susan guides her to the nearby chair.

"You should sit for a minute, Mary Jo. Just take your time. Nathan, can you get her some water?"

I don't want Mom to take her time to explain what is going on, but I sit down next to her and try to wait patiently. After Mr. Landry returns with the water in a tiny paper cup, she sips from it, then reaches over to give my hand a squeeze.

"The police are questioning Max about Friday night. They think he may know something about the murder at the quarry. The one you and Mr. Hanover investigated Saturday morning."

"So, it isn't about the vandalism?"

"Do they know who it was, yet?"

Kayla and I blurt out our questions at the same time.

Mom looks first at me, confused, but shakes her head no before nodding affirmatively to Kayla.

"Yes, the police have released the little girl's name. Victoria Small. I don't know who that is, but it's been officially announced now. Something about the parents being separated and custody issues—that's why nobody realized she was missing until it was…too late." Mom's eyes fill with tears. "Max is not under arrest. They have been questioning him, because they found his phone this morning in the field below the quarry. The one he uses to cut back and forth for work. The police want to know if he saw or heard anything."

"Did he? Did he see or hear anyone?" Kayla asks loudly. It's obvious she wants the killer caught.

"No. Max was so intent on getting home and then trying to find his phone after he lost it, he says he wasn't even paying attention."

"Do they believe him?" I ask, a feeling of dread coming over me. "The police don't…they don't think he had anything to do with her death, do they? Do they?"

I could see clearly why they would see him as a potential suspect. Teenage boy with a family history of mental illness who is currently being treated for it? Works at the local activity center where young girls are known to frequent? Admits to being in the nearby area of the latest murder in a series of murders? Crap, I would look at all of this circumstantial evidence and want to investigate him myself.

"They do. I think." Mom takes another sip of her water. "The investigators seemed rough on him at first. I guess so he would cooperate. Now they just seem to want as much information from him as they can get."

"That's good!" Susan exclaims. "The idea of someone like Max being the Floating Angels Murderer is simply ridiculous. He loves helping others too much to hurt someone."

We all nod in agreement. I stand back up. I can't sit still thinking about what these people have been saying to my brother.

"They looked his clothes and shoes over pretty good. I think the investigators may have found something like that at the scene." Mom rubs her hair again. "Maybe I shouldn't have let them do that." She turns to Mr. Landry. "Susan's told me you're a good lawyer. Would you be willing to advise me on something? I can pay you."

Mr. Landry extends his hand for her to shake. "Please Mary Jo, call me Nathan. Susan talks so often about you, and the boys, too, that I feel like I know everyone. I don't practice juvenile law, but I can answer general questions. If you need more advice, I can recommend a colleague."

Mom smiles weakly. "Thank you. The police have asked if Max will voluntarily provide a DNA sample to prove that he was not involved. I want to know if that is a good idea or not."

"May I ask why you would want your son to do that? It doesn't sound as though the police are suspicious of Max, or they would be going for a court order."

"They aren't, but they asked if he would be willing. So there would be no question of his involvement at the scene. I want it clear that he's had nothing to do with what's happened to this little girl."

"Mary Jo, very few lawyers would ever advise a client to voluntarily offer anything that can be used for evidence unless a court order has been obtained requesting it." Mr. Landry drops down in my former chair to lean in toward my mother.

"I understand." Mom looks troubled. "But there's something else the detectives warned me about before I came out here. Something that is really going to be hard for Max to handle once we leave this building."

We wait for the blow.

Mom takes a deep breath and squares her shoulders. She is in full warrior mother mode and prepared to defend her child at all costs.

"Someone leaked to the press that Max is a person of interest in these crimes. Right now there is a whole parking lot of television crews and reporters waiting outside to crucify my son. I can't let that happen." She wrings her hands. "My…Max isn't strong enough to have everyone out there thinking he's capable of killing those little girls."

Mom's right. Max isn't. All that attention. Reporters asking him to comment on being a killer. He cares too much about helping others to accept being branded a murderer.

"Maybe it won't be so bad, Mary Jo. The police can have a news conference and clear his name," Susan says quickly.

"Even if they do, it won't matter. Madison is a small town, and although there's good people living here too, I haven't forgotten what it was like when Mike died. The rumors…the veiled comments that I was somehow responsible. Max doesn't deserve that."

"Neither did you, Mary Jo." Susan stares earnestly at her best friend's face.

Mom reaches over and clasps Susan's hand. "I know that. Now. But it was upsetting." She shifts back around in her chair to face Mr. Landry. "But if I've learned anything from my husband's death, it is that the truth doesn't matter as much a rumor. If the police do the DNA test, it would prove Max had nothing to do with the crime and it might make it easier for him."

Mr. Landry is already shaking his head no, before Mom finishes. "It won't work, Mary Jo. It's not like in the movies where they do the test swabs and immediately find out the results. It could be weeks or months before they know the results. That won't help Max in time."

I smack my fist into my other hand. "So there's nothing we can do for him. This sucks!" My words echo in the large waiting area and Kayla comes over and hugs me. I put my hands inside the front pocket of my purple hoodie that she wears and hold her close. I breathe in her comforting girl scent deeply and try to calm down. Mom has enough to contend with, without me freaking out too.

Kayla leans back, looks at the lawyer and asks tentatively, "What happens if the police run the tests and they made Max look guilty?"

"What?" I jerk my hands back and stand face to face with her. "How can you even say that about Max?"

Does Kayla really think my brother could be the killer? That's impossible. Isn't it?

Isn't it?

It has to be!

Kayla bursts into tears from me yelling at her. "I just meant…what if Max came into contact with the little girl or her clothes somehow? Would that show up on the test?" Kayla takes a ragged breath and wipes her face off with the sleeve of my purple hoodie. She can keep it now, for sure. "I'm sorry, I don't know how stuff like that works."

She looks at me for forgiveness and I give her nothing. I'm too angry. Part of it could be anger at myself for allowing her questions to bring up my own doubts.

I go sit next to Mom. She seems to have no questions about Max's innocence.

"It's unlikely that Max's fingerprints or DNA would be transferred to this girl's clothing through casual contact, if he even knew her. But, they are making inroads every day in the area of trace DNA. One cell may be all they need. My advice is still no samples, but I can call someone in if you like." Mr. Landry offers.

I like Susan's attorney boyfriend. He keeps trying to help us.

"That's not necessary. I'll take your advice and we won't bother with the test unless the police come back and insist." Mom sounds sure of this decision.

"I think you're right. It most likely would have upset Max to have to be swabbed for DNA evidence." Susan pats Mom's shoulder.

"They said he's almost done, so I'm going back in there and telling them it's a no on the testing. I think they'll let him go."

"Let me arrange to bring your car around to the back door. That way we can miss that group outside. If it's okay with you, Mary Jo, I'll drive you and Max home. Susan and the rest of you can meet me there and she can bring me back here later for my car. "

Mom looks like she is about to refuse, but finally nods. It isn't easy for her to accept help. She's used to taking care of her boys on her own.

"Well, I am going to grab some fried chicken and sides from the drive-thru and going over to your house to wait. I remember where the key is hidden." Susan is already pulling on her jacket. "Kayla, you can ride with me. Marty?"

I don't even have to look at my girlfriend to know what she wants me to do. But there's no way I'm going anywhere without my brother.

"I'll wait for Max."

I look over at Mom, who smiles. She probably expects this from me, the protective older twin.

I smile back at her. I suddenly remember a fact in a lesson about DNA from my seventh grade science class.

"Did you guys know if Max couldn't give a sample that I can do it for him?"

Everyone looks curiously at me.

"Max and I are identical twins. We have exactly the same DNA. If the test came back with a positive, I would look just as guilty."

That's right little doggie, you like this, don't you? Friendly guy, aren't you? Keep gobbling it up.

Good thing my old lady watches the pet channel. Told me all about how dogs being allergic. And this is so easy, isn't it? Just stop at the convenience store for a few supplies, and we're good to go. Don't worry, boy. You can have all of these chocolate bars you want.

Police won't put your owner in jail for killing all those girls? So, you get to pay for your owner being a murderer.

You guys about done trashing the house? It will be light soon. Yeah, he ate everything I bought. Good dog.

Unnamed Dog Poisoner

27

I roll over in my bed and lean up to look at the clock. It's after 1:00 AM and I still can't sleep tonight. Thor and the other neighborhood dogs have been restless tonight. They keep barking back and forth every so often. Probably the wind or a cat or something out by our dog's kennel or maybe an opossum. Thor hates it when they get in the trashcans. I turn in my bed to look over at Max. I can't really see much in the darkness, but his soft breathing tells me he isn't disturbed by the noise. That's good. He's not snoring, even though Mom gave him the new medicine to help him sleep. She's had to give him something more often in the weeks since we were at the police station.

I hate not being able to sleep. I almost wish Max would wake up, so we can do the robot story. I can pretend it's to comfort him, but the truth is that I could use it too. Since Max was questioned about the death of the little girl, Victoria Small, we might need to change the story's last refrain from, *TOGETHER forever* to *ALONE together.* My brother and I may end up that way yet.

The reaction of the community to Victoria Small's death has been just as Mom suspected. Max's a pariah and Mom and I are, too, by association. Doesn't matter that Max was only questioned as a witness. Doesn't even matter that Cy published an article with a quote from the Chief of Police that stated that fact. Nope, public opinion is that my brother drowns little girls.

Each week, our problems increase. The activity center fired Max first thing. Reporters are always trying to catch us on our way into the house to ask questions. Our car got keyed at the grocery store. We aren't even able to walk Thor around the block. Somebody threw beer bottles out of a truck the last time Max and Mom tried. She has a real fear someone will drive by and try to shoot one of us.

School is the worst. Students and even some of the teachers won't talk to me, especially the ones who think I am Max. If not for Kayla, Ray, Claire and Billy I would go through the whole day without people talking to me.

Even Max isn't there. Principal Morris arranged for him to be homeschooled, after the second time someone started punching on him. I got the same offer to stay home, but I refused. I'm willing to fight for my right to be there. Besides, I have something more important to worry about than problems at school.

For the first time in our lives, I'm truly afraid for Max's emotional health. He is deeply depressed. I don't blame him. It's hard having a whole town think you're a killer. But I remember enough from how Dad acted right before he killed himself to know Max is acting a lot like that now. And I'm not alone in noticing it. The doctor touches base regularly trying to adjust his meds. Mrs. Applewhite stays with Max during the day while Mom and I are out. We just can't leave him alone. The risk is too great.

The bedroom door opens slowly, blinding me momentarily from the small light in the kitchen we always leave on at night. I'm not the only family member awake tonight.

"Hi, Mom," I whisper softly.

"I was hoping you were already asleep. Sorry," Mom says softly, coming in the room. She peers over at Max. In the dim light from the doorway, he looks so innocent.

There's a word we haven't heard much of recently.

I sit up and slide my feet out of the way for her to sit. The bed dips as she perches on the edge. I inhale the comforting essence that is my mother. It's some kind of floral and vanilla scent that always permeates the air around her. I remember burying my face in her neck as a kid just to smell it.

"Is anything wrong?" Mom asks. Even in the dim light I can see the chagrin on her face at asking a question with such an evident answer. "I mean, besides the obvious."

"Just the usual crap from people who think my brother is a murderer," I add darkly. "And that I'm him." It isn't bad enough that Max gets persecuted as a *Person of Interest* in the Floating Angels Murders, but I get the same treatment. That whole 'identical' thing strikes again.

I feel guilty for my words and thoughts, and more so, when Mom doesn't respond for a moment.

"I'm sorry I said that, Mom."

"I'm sorry about this, Marty."

Both statements come out at the same time and then it's silent.

"Neither of us need to apologize. We aren't the problem. Him either." I nod toward Max.

"Not everyone is against us, you know." Mom slides back closer to me. "Nana and Papa, Kayla and her family, my friends at the hospital, some of your teachers and the counselors. Even Principal Morris has been helpful. I think the Applewhites feel almost as bad as we do."

"Yeah Mom, but how many more hate us?"

"Too many, Marty. Too many." Mom's own doubt about the goodness of people shows.

"You got that right."

My doubt is not in question.

"Still, we've got our supporters." The bed shakes as Mom sits up straight. "Want to hear a funny story?"

"More than I can say."

"Today, while you were still working at the paper, that obnoxious reporter was outside doing a report by the driveway."

"The blonde one on Channel 6 who won't leave us alone?"

Just a guess. There are so many options of obnoxious reporters to choose from.

"Yes, that one. Well, Thelma told me that Mr. Applewhite was rinsing off their car with the hose when the reporter and cameraman pulled up. Once they were set up and ready to broadcast, Mr. Applewhite *accidentally* lost control of the hose and drenched both of them and their remote camera equipment."

Mom voice's rich with laughter as she leans in to nudge my shoulder with hers. "She screeched like a howling monkey and her hair was a flat mess."

I can't help it. I grin in the dark. "I wish I had that on tape." Seeing that woman looking like a wet dog would go viral.

"The best part was that when she tried to yell at Mr. Applewhite. Then he claimed to have a weak heart. He threatened to call the government and turn in the station for elder abuse."

I choke, trying to keep a deep laugh in. Mr. Applewhite might be in his eighties, but the word *weak* is not a part of the man in any way, shape, or even in his form.

"Mrs. Applewhite chased them back to their van with her dish towel."

My sides now hurt from trying to laugh quietly. I hear a dog bark outside.

"I'll bet that reporter hated her bath as much as Thor does."

Since Thor is hilarious when trying to get out of taking a bath, we both giggle. We immediately still when Max moves restlessly in his bed. Once we're assured he's back to sleep, Mom stands up. She needs her rest too, even though she has less to do now that she's on leave from her college classes.

"Get some sleep, Sweetheart. Our family is going to make it through this." Mom turns to leave and I look over where my brother rests. I know she hears me whisper, "TOGETHER forever."

"Boys! Get up." I am shoved hard and I open my eyes to see Mom doing the same to Max.

I sit up. "What? It's Saturday, isn't it?"

Max is struggling just to get his eyes open and I hope my hair isn't sticking out as badly as his. I put my hand up to feel. It is. Maybe even worse.

"Hurry up. Get dressed." Mom has the dresser drawer open and is throwing clothes towards us. It's weird she's so insistent, since she's still wearing her pajamas and her bathrobe. "Now, Max. Move!"

Something must be bad for her to use that tone with him. She's knows how hard he has to struggle to wake up. I squint out the window and can tell it's barely daylight.

"Mom?" She's halfway out the bedroom door when she turns and I see the tears running down her face. "What is it?"

She swallows. "It's Thor. Someone's poisoned him and we have to get him to the vet now or it will be too—"

She doesn't even get the word *late* out before Max and I are out of our beds crashing into each other trying to pull some pants on. We grab shirts and our jackets and shoes from the porch. It's the first time my younger brother ever beat me out the door in the morning.

"We'll just have to wait and see. His heart may be compromised and we need to monitor these seizures. From the numbers of wrappers you brought in, it's obvious Thor's ingested a large amount. I'm sorry, but his prognosis is not looking good."

I drop my head even closer toward my chest as Max moans loudly from the chair where he slumps close to Mom.

Dr. Grimaldi squats down in front of my twin. This is the vet who always helps when Max brings in an animal, and the guy who regularly treats Thor. He knows our dog is family to us.

"Max, I promise you that we will give Thor the very best care we can give him." The doctor stares at Max. "You know that, right?" After a few seconds Max nods and the doctor stands up. "Now, I suggest you all go on home. I promise to call with any updates and you all can come later this evening and check in on him if you like."

"I want to stay." I knew Max would say that. We all expected it.

Dr. Grimaldi shrugs, "You're welcome to stay, but it's going to be rough and you have to be ready for the worst. Do you understand that, Max?"

My brother set his jaw and nodded.

"Okay. I'm going in the back and you can discuss this as a family. Either way, I'll keep you informed."

Max and I look at Mom who's already shaking her head no before the man leaves the reception area. "Honey, you heard the doctor. He'll call us and we can come back. I need to get into the hospital, and Marty's late for work, too." Mom bit her lip. "Max, you have to go to the house to take your medicine. Your levels…"

"Is this how it's going to be my whole life?" Max's voice breaks and the sound of his anguish is like someone just gave me a hard punch to my chest. "Am I always going to worry so much about taking my meds that I can't be there for the ones who count on me?" Max's grabs Mom's hand. "Thor needed me last night. He needed me to protect him…and I was too doped up to wake up and help him. Now he's probably going to die. What use am I to him…to anyone?"

"Oh, son." Mom bursts into tears. "Please, please don't say that. Don't feel that. That's how your dad felt before…"

The silence echoes between us. We all knew the rest of this sentence.

"I understand why Dad did it—what happened in his garage. Do you, Mom? Marty? Do you guys understand what it's like to know that you're probably always going to need someone to help you? To check on you, to make sure you take your meds, that you aren't too hyper or too sad, and that you don't kill yourself? That you can't even depend on yourself to be well enough to be there for the ones you love, because you're sick?" Max slumps in his chair. "Because I live with it every single day, and I can't face myself if I can't be here for Thor. If all I can ever be is someone else's burden."

Mom's face is white under the tears running down. Max looks up at me bleakly and I want to help him. To help Mom.

"He isn't Dad, Mom. He's not hiding in his room refusing to admit there's a problem. Refusing to take his meds." I shake with the anger toward my father that seeps out. Maybe I'm not the best person to help Max make his case, after all. I breathe out slowly and try again. "Even with all of this crap over the Floating Angels Murders, Max tries to be better, to be well." I rock back and forth on my feet and wait for my mother's response. She stares blankly at Max, so I try again. "The doctor said he could stay with Thor. I know he's just a dog, but he's mostly Max's dog."

"And what if *his* dog dies?" Mom takes Max's hand in her own. "Are you strong enough to watch that?"

My brother sits up straight in his chair and I swear I see him grow up in front of my eyes.

"I'd rather watch Thor die and be there for him than to live knowing I let him down."

Silence.

"Okay." Mom sits upright in her own chair and begins wiping up her face. "You can stay, but I'm going home to get your medication and something for you to eat before I call the police to make a report about this. Marty, what about you?"

"You can take me home to get my phone, and then you'd better drop me off at the newspaper office on your way back here. I was supposed to be at work an hour and a half ago." I pull my hoodie on and stick my fist out toward Max to pound. "Take good care of Thor. You've got this."

For once, I really do believe that my younger, bipolar brother does.

I've been keeping my eyes and ears open to find out what kind of evidence the police found up at the quarry. So far nobody's talking, but I already put most of the stuff I wore that day in one of those clothing bins they've placed around town. I can't imagine what else might tie me to Victoria.

I know that police are really suspicious of everybody right now, but I can't stop. Too many girls in Madison need my help. Too many get let down by people who say they love them.

I'm going to be there for them, no matter what the police think.

The Killer

I slam my camera bag down on my desk and flop in the chair before sucking in some hard breaths. I blow them all out at once. I finally made it to work, but I'm so angry I can barely function.

What is wrong with people?

It's bad enough Thor's poisoned and still may die. But did they have to trash the front of our home last night too?

The first clue Mom and I had about this came from the police car parked outside the house. We'd been so focused on Thor when we left, we hadn't even noticed the new paint job. Once it got light enough to see, the Applewhites called the police about the hate messages sprawled all across the front of our home. On the upside, Mom got to report what had happened to Thor sooner than she planned. The police took the report, but didn't seem too hopeful that anyone would be arrested. Too many possibilities of people who hate Jamisons. Another downside of this day? It's still too cold in February to paint outside. Lucky us. We get to keep the hate decorations until it warms up. I finally just grabbed my stuff and headed for the office.

I hear Cy moving in his office. He's most likely working on another story about the Floating Angels Murders. It's been his focus for weeks, but I know that he isn't any closer to determining the killer's true identity than I am when I write up the minutes from the school board meetings. Besides, who needs anyone to solve the Floating Angels Murders? They have my brother to blame, our family dog to poison, and our house to defile.

I sigh. Maybe I should have stayed home, but I just couldn't stay there knowing that crap is covering the house. I'd thought about going over to see Kayla for a while, but she's busy today babysitting for one of the doctors who works with my mom.

"Why don't you come in here, son?"

Cy stands in the doorway of his office. The fact that he didn't bellow like normal means he already knows something happened before I got here.

"Okay." I answer sullenly before following him in. I watch him shut the door. Just great. The way my life has been going, he's probably going to fire me for being late. He indicates the chair with his head and I sit down across the desk from him.

"Your mother called."

"Figured. Was it to say that the vet couldn't do anything and Thor's dead?" I try to sound like I don't care, but I'm not successful.

"No, but she told me everything that's happened."

"You mean your contacts didn't give you the scoop? How we Jamisons are the scourge of Madison, MO? You could write a whole story with the title, "Death by Chocolate for Crazed Killer's Dog." Perfect title, just full of alliteration and a message to please the readers. Or how about, "Local Family Receives House Improvements." It's not quite as snappy, but I could get a nice shot of the painted figure whose head gets cut off. I'm pretty sure it was supposed to represent Max, but who knows? We would still look just alike even decapitated. Irony, uh?"

I can't help this fountain of bitterness from pouring out, and I slam my fist on my knee a couple of times.

After a minute of no response from my boss, I look up to see him studying me.

"Kid, I think you really need a drink." Cy reaches over and pulls open his bottom desk drawer with the liquor.

Is he actually giving me one? Is that why he closed the door? I don't even think I'll like whiskey.

Cy takes the cap off and pours a good amount of the brown liquid.

"Of course, you aren't old enough and I would hate to upset your dear mother, so I'll drink one on your behalf." He puts the glass up to his lips, throws it back, wipes his mouth with the back of his hand, and sets the glass and the bottle back in the drawer.

"How is that supposed to help me?" I ask, irritated that he wasted my time and the glare I give him backs this up. There's enough people in Madison, Missouri, treating me badly that I don't need Cy being a smart...aleck. My mother taught me to be respectful of the elderly, so I'll stick with that word for now.

"Makes it easier for me to put up with you."

I seethe, "Can I just go back to my computer and write a stupid story about crop predictions or old ladies discussing which tulip bulbs will be the hardiest this spring or something else useless like that?" I get up to stomp out.

Cy sends me back into my seat with a single word command. "Sit!"

He's never actually raised his voice to me before. Maybe I should have skipped the hateful tone of my question. I really do want to work at the newspaper. It's just been a really, really bad day.

"How old are you, boy?"

"Fifteen, at least for another week." Who knows what this has to do with anything?

"Is that when you get a regular driving license that lets you drive without your momma along?"

Someone at the office ratted me out about not being old enough to drive without a parent after my illegal trips to and from the quarry.

"Yes, if I pass my driving test. Max is waiting awhile before taking his test, but Mom's taking me on the morning of our birthdays. Why?"

"I ask the questions here, young man," Cy barks at me.

It's going to look so bad on my future college applications if I really am fired today.

"Jamison, do you want this trouble to end with your family?" Cy leans in closer across his desk toward me.

"Wouldn't you?"

"I would." He stares intently. "Okay, starting right now, you are promoted from intern to junior investigative reporter. We are going to investigate these murders together. Everything I know, you'll know too. Maybe you can see something in the files that the rest of us have missed."

"So we might be able to determine the real killer and my family won't be treated like crap anymore?" I lean up in my chair and am nearly nose to nose with Cy. "No more deaths threats and having people I've known my whole life refusing to talk to me?"

"Well, I can't promise anything, but we can try. Son, some of what you're going to see and hear will be rough. There's photos." Cy lifts the pile of file folders full of his information on the Floating Angels Murders in his hands. "Do you think you're ready for this?"

A chance to clear my twin's name? To find the real killer and stop more little girls from drowning? To be a real reporter and end all of the hate for my family? Sounds good, but first a little fun.

I'm about to say an enthusiastic yes when I decide to pay my boss back for some of the pranks he's pulled on me. I lean back in my chair casually putting my arms above my head with my hands locked together behind my neck. "Well Cy, I guess that depends."

His eyebrow raises in question.

"How much more am I going to be paid with this promotion?"

Cy's eyes narrow and he stared at me with the gaze of a gritty Old West gunslinger.

"Not one stinking dime."

"Perfect." I reach across the desk and put my hands on the other end of the files. "You better freaking believe I'm ready for this."

It can be difficult to pinpoint the events in a person's background that create a killer.

For some serial killers, the crimes are re-creations of a past traumatic event or a series of them. Common indicators are physical or sexual abuse, death of family members, or emotional isolation from primary caregivers. Weak victims, such as the young girls in the current murders, may simply provide easier opportunities to have control, or it could be that their youth is the trigger.

Whether the individuals were the actual victims or powerless bystanders in the original trauma, they seek to manufacture duplicate scenarios where they can be in control. Possibly to find revenge or to provide the aid they were unable to before. However, the circumstances of the original trauma can never be replicated exactly, so true satisfaction or peace is never achieved. Thus, the individual is driven to seek more victims or more opportunities to achieve emotional peace.

Rarely, do they simply give up. The drive to kill again is still within them.

Elena King-Psychologist

29

"Mom said to tell you that we're leaving for the bowling alley in fifteen minutes." Max sticks his head into our bedroom to deliver the message. "I'm taking Thor over to stay with the Applewhites while we're at the party."

"Okay. Tell them thanks for taking care of him." Thor has been doing great since he recovered from the poisoning, but we don't ever leave him unsupervised. Even when we're going to our sixteenth birthday party.

"I will, because I am going over there. One of us saying thank you is enough." Max is in Mr. Literal mood again. It was too much to hope that age sixteen would be the magic number to make that stop.

I guess it could be worse. Since that day at the vet's office, Max has been doing a lot better. He's not back in school yet, because people still hate him. But he is noticeably happier and more confident since he was able to be there for his friend.

I look at the papers and files covering my bed and wish that I had some confidence that Cy and I will ever figure out anything about the identity of the true Floating Angels Murderer. We've both studied transcripts of interviews, crime scene photos and notes, and made list after list of evidence to try and find a pattern in the lives of the victims that would make them appealing to the serial killer. I've been reviewing my lists too. I look down at the next one.

Natalee P, Lola R, Peggy C, Victoria S.

Similarities

About the same age. (Not uncommon for serial killers.)

Attend Madison Elementary. (Everyone who lives in Madison does.)

Physical builds are slight. (Probably because they're easier to overpower.)

Participate in activities within the town, but not necessarily the same ones. (Dance, Basketball, T-Ball, Art and Crafts)

Bodies found wearing variety of colors and styles of girl's clothing. (Shirts, pants, pajamas, socks, jewelry, hair stuff…and a lot of underwear with princesses on them.)

Differences

Don't all have the same hair or eye color.

Not of the same economic group.

No consistency in teachers, bus drivers, coaches, doctors, or restaurants, churches, stores.

Did not appear to know each other.

What we know

No patterns evident among the girls.

Not enough to convince people Max is innocent.

Not enough to keep another one from being killed.

That these are the same conclusions I reach each time I go over my notes.

And that this really, really sucks.

"The final pin is down! And that's the ball game, folks."

Billy yells out the result of our bowling match by mixing up the sport terms in his commentary. Then he performs a horrendous arm pumping, butt shaking victory dance. It certainly isn't a pretty sight, but it makes all of us laugh. We all roar when Billy's enthusiastic strike celebration combines with his large lineman build and the bowling alley's waxy floor to send him crashing down.

Barely able to breathe from laughter, Ray and Max haul the bowling legend up and he limps off to the side to seek comfort from his girlfriend Jenna. She's the real reason their team won. She's a great bowler with the sense to celebrate a win without employing Billy's wild gyrating moves.

It's been a great afternoon in spite of my earlier frustration over not getting anywhere with determining the true killer. I think Mom's still a little disappointed we didn't have more people here to celebrate our birthdays other than Cindy, Susan, Mr. Landry, Kayla, and our friends, Ray, Billy, and Jenna. She's invited more, but most people just didn't show up. I'm pretty sure Claire would have come if I invited her, but I didn't. I wasn't sure how Kayla would react. She'd been really moody recently.

Maybe she's still getting flack for dating me or there could be problems at home with her mom again. Hard to tell.

"So, are we going another round? I'm pretty sure Max and I could take you this time." Ray has his florescent ball in hand, striking his best bowling intimidation stance.

"Son, you and Max came in dead last every game you played. Maybe you better rest that arm for the upcoming baseball season." Cy is shaking his head in disgust at Ray's flippant attitude. I snicker, because it's obvious that my boss takes his bowling very seriously. It's the matching customized bag, ball, shoes, shirt, and personalized towel that gives it away.

"Good point. Season's not here yet, but I'd hate to hurt it when I've got my big date with the senior coming up."

Ray claims he has a date next week with a girl that we've all heard has a tattoo in an interesting area. I'll believe it when I see it. That Ray goes out with the girl, I mean. Not the tattoo. I'm too happy with my own girl today to worry about another one's tattoo placement. I smile over at Kayla, who is talking to Billy and Jenna.

"Everyone, why don't you go ahead and change into your street shoes. The pizza's here and we still have cake and presents." Mom hurries off to the streamer and balloon-decorated party room. The other adults follow once they take care of their bowling shoes.

Mom says not everyone hates our family and I guess she's right. One of the doctors she works with owns the bowling alley. When he heard Mom was looking for a place for our sixteenth birthday party, he had insisted on us using it, and wouldn't even take money. Said he was tired of our family continuing to be harassed. Kayla told me that he and his wife are nice like that. She babysits for them sometimes.

"Hey Kayla, you need me to carry those clown shoes up to the counter for you?" Ray asks in fake tone of caring.

Kayla shared earlier in the day how she hates bowling shoes because they show the person's size on the heel. She thinks her feet are big for a girl.

I watch to see how she takes Ray's jab.

"What if I toss my shoes to you and they hit your head? It might knock what little is in there loose. Then you'd probably forget you have a date with Miss Nasty Tattoo, and whatever would you do?"

Apparently, my girl can handle Ray like a champion. We all laugh and throw our own shoes at Ray. Max gamely helps him pick them up and they take off with them toward the check-in counter.

"That pizza smells good. Dibs on the pepperoni and sausage!" Billy grabs Jenna's hand and drags her along a little in his enthusiasm.

I finish tying my last shoe and am ready to go grab a piece of the pepperoni and sausage for myself when I realize that I'm something I haven't truly been in a long time. Happy. Smiley, deep down, happy-face-emoticon, happy. It's been so long since I felt this way that I almost don't recognize the feeling.

I stand up and start to help Kayla into the purple hoodie. I can see Max across the room and he looks over at me and smiles. Without a word between us I know we are both thinking that it's a great day to celebrate. Together.

"Do you want me to hold that birthday cash in my wallet for you? I don't want you to strain yourself," Max offers.

Sometimes Max says goofy stuff like this because he is so literal, but I know he's repeating a dumb joke our grandfather used to make when we were kids and got money for a gift. Papa did it up until the point his Alzheimer's made him forget us. Sad reminder, but I appreciate that Max feels good enough to joke.

Most everyone is busy helping clean up from the party, so we can turn the bowling alley over to the manager for the evening leagues. The ladies pack up the leftover cake and supplies while the rest of us dispose of the trash and decorations. Cy and Susan's boyfriend Nathan Landry sit in the corner sharing war stories of the court system.

Before I can answer, Kayla sneaks up and grabs the money before tucking it in the front pocket of the purple hoodie. She then drapes herself over me from the back and that's a pretty good birthday present all by itself.

"That's okay, Max. I'm sure Marty will let me take this money and pick out something nice for him." Kayla nuzzles the back of my ear with her lips, and I'm ready to hand over my birthday money and about half my clothes too, even in our mixed company. Man, I love getting along with my girlfriend even more than having a birthday.

Max clears his throat and rolls his eyes. "Wise men say the path to happiness takes a village. So put that money in my hut."

"Don't you mean your hat? Do you ever take that thing off?"

Kayla refers to the knitted hat Max got at the activity center. He rarely takes it off, and I know for a fact that he wears it in bed, too.

"Nope, I can't afford a comb. That's why I want some of Marty's money too, so I can get some nice ones." Max pulls his hat tighter on his head. "Don't worry, I'll leave enough with Marty in case you want to borrow some cash to buy more big, ugly shoes."

I first think Mr. Literal has struck again, but I notice the barely-there quiver of my twin's upper lip. Good one, bro.

Kayla, however, has not figured out Max is teasing. She's giving him the death glare over my shoulder. Talk about moody.

I slide my arms up inside the loose armholes of the jacket and squeeze her in closer to me. "It's a joke, babe." We're still attached when she gives her head a shake and her body relaxes.

"Wise girl says money is not the path to happiness. It's helping others out like this." She nuzzles my neck and gives me a squeeze around my middle. "Right, Marty?"

I smile the cocky smile of a young man in like, lust, and maybe even some love. "Heck yeah."

Ray and Billy make loud gagging sounds together on cue as if they had practiced.

Kayla and I laugh. I look over and notice that Max isn't laughing. He's standing perfectly still just staring either at us or behind. Intently. It's weird. I glance back for a quick look and don't see anything unusual. Must be jealous I have such a protective hot girlfriend and he doesn't.

Ring, Ring, Ring

Everyone pauses and looks around the group to see whose phone is ringing. It's Cy. He pulls his cell out of his pocket and starts trying to answer it. Technology like a cell phone is too much for the man, so I disengage from Kayla and head over to him. I already know from experience he can't turn it on without his glasses. I push the appropriate areas and hand it back, and turn to head back to cleaning.

"Hello."

"Say that again…. When?... They sure?... What's the name?... They found what?... Okay, okay I'll be right there." Cy's volume increases with everything he says until he's yelling so loudly that everyone in the room is staring, curious to see what has him so excited.

Cy shoves his phone in the pocket of his shirt pocket, grabs his bowling bag, and stands. He realizes we are all waiting to know what he learned in the call. He looks directly at me.

"Son, you and I are going to have to leave this party a little early. We've got a story to write. A good one."

"How good?" I scoot over for Max who has come up beside me.

"Outstanding. Are you two ready to get the best birthday present you'll ever get in your lives?" Cy is definitely smiling. "Police just brought in a suspect for the murders. According to my source, he's a good one too. Said he was wearing the shoes that match the prints they got up at the quarry. Had a bunch of little girl and women's clothes in his room." Cy's face is practically cracking, because he smiles so broadly. "Boys, I think this is the guy."

The actual Floating Angels Murderer in police custody? Our family's nightmare of Max being falsely accused by the public over?

I don't know what Max wished for on his birthday candles this year, but I just got *exactly* what I wanted.

I just can't believe you and Burl, Jr. didn't hear about this Floating Angels Murders down there in Poplar Bluff. Your news stations must not be worth a dang.

Well, it was just like I said in my letter. His name was Rudolph Coleman, and if that last name don't tell you something about that man's cold heart, I don't know what would.

Paper said he was renting a room in one of them boarding houses. I've always said them boarding houses is just a breeding ground for druggies, devil worshippers, and serial killers. And I was right as rain about that.

Anyhoo, this fellow was a janitor at one of them gym places for kids. The police picked up that girl-killer Coleman at that gym still a'wearing the shoes he wore when he threw that last one down in the rock quarry. Poor little angel.

Betty, have you and your Burl, Jr. got your garden in yet? It's been too wet this spring to get much in the ground up here.

Florence Hobbs-Madison resident

30

"So did you ever see the guy trying to talk to the little girls?" It's a few nights after our joint birthday party, and I'm in my bed talking across the darkness with Max.

Every time I've seen my brother the last couple of days I ask more questions about Rudy Coleman, his friend from the activity center. He's the guy now officially charged with being Victoria Small's killer and is still under investigation for the deaths of the Cotton and Reyes girls, and probably Natalee's, too. I do know from working on this week's stories with Cy that the people of Madison we interviewed think he is guilty of all of the Floating Angels Murders. Even the experts think it's only a matter of time before he's indicted for all of them.

"Everybody that works at the activity center talked to little girls and big ones and boys and men, too. It's part of the job description."

"What else did he tell you about his background in Savannah? Did he mention the niece that turned him in?" I smile, knowing I'm becoming more like Cy in my instigative reporting skills.

Nobody would be asking any questions of Rudolph Coleman if his niece didn't watch those unsolved murder shows. She'd recognized Rudy in a piece filmed at the activity center and contacted police. She claimed that her family disowned the man because he got caught stealing her clothes when she was younger. Investigators here in Missouri looked into her tip and found an old juvenile record of peeping at young women back in Georgia. His history, previous record, and the shoes he was wearing that matched the print from the crime scene made him indictment worthy. The room full of kid's clothing they found in his room at the boarding house didn't help him much, either.

"Max?"

"Would you please stop interviewing me? You're being a jerk!" I hear the thud in the dark as Max kicks the wall turning away from me.

I'm a jerk? Because I am relieved and excited that the real killer has been found and want to make sure he goes away for a very long time? That all of the crap over the perception that Max had something to do with the crimes can now be behind us? That my life can go back to being normal now? Hardly.

"I'd think you'd be happy to do anything you could to see that this guy pays for what happened to those girls. You're the one of us who always *helps* everyone and everything." I huff. "Or do you just not care about your friend Jacob getting some justice for what happened to Natalee anymore?"

Nothing.

I curse under my breath and roll over to face the wall too.

"Of course I care about what happened. I just have a hard time accepting that Rudy killed those girls." I hear Max roll over and sit up. "He was always so nice to me. Even after the activity center fired me, he'd call here to check on me. And he gave me the hat."

Max loves that stupid hat. After him wearing it pretty much non-stop for the last couple of months, it now sits unused on the top of our dresser.

Maybe Max is right, I am being a jerk. The knitted hat is more than something to hide his messy hair for him, and Coleman is more than just an accused killer to him. He had been Max's friend. I roll over and sit up too.

"Yeah, but that doesn't mean he didn't do this," I say quietly.

"I get that and if he killed the girls, I want him to be punished for it. But how can he be so nice to me and so horrible at the same time? It doesn't make sense."

I don't have an answer for this. In fact, these murders have reminded me that there often isn't a perfect explanation when it comes to people's actions.

"Maybe we all have good and bad in us and it's more of a struggle for some people to choose a good path."

"Like Dad." Max's voice is soft when he mentions the "D" word. He knows the subject can trigger my own anger.

"He wasn't really bad, but he didn't choose a good path."

"No, he didn't. I think him being bipolar and refusing treatment took over control of his path. Before that guy embezzled all of the money from their garage and Dad had to shut it down, he was a good guy. Remember how he was?"

Max is right. Dad had been a loving husband and father until he allowed his illness to take control. I let out a breath I hadn't even realized I was holding.

"I don't see how Rudy Coleman deciding to kill all of those girls is like Dad," I say.

"Maybe Rudy started out a good guy, but something in his life got messed up. It changed him. Made him choose to take a bad path."

"Maybe."

Our clock in the living room lets out a faint chime. It's getting late. I lean back and slide down in the bed. "We need to get to sleep. Driving test tomorrow, and I intend to pass the first time."

"Mom says I need to wait a couple of weeks to get more practice in." The bed rustles as Max settles in.

We lay in the quiet and wait for sleep to take over.

"Things will be better for us now, right Marty?"

"Yes, I think they will. Finally."

"Jamison, when you get that story on the Elementary Spring Carnival filed, come in here. I need to talk to you," Cy orders from the depths of his office.

I get up out of my desk chair and head in. My boss is standing at his window staring out at the parking lot. He turns and motions for me to sit before shutting the office door and sitting down in his own chair. He peers at me, his features arranged in a sober manner that screams something serious is about to happen.

"Kid, sometimes the time comes for a person to move on."

Oh man, am I getting fired? Sure, things have been slow while we wait for Coleman to be scheduled for trial, but I've been doing good work. I think. I brace myself for whatever comes next.

"Today is one of those times." Cy leans back in his chair. He's awfully casual to be firing me.

"You got a dollar on you?"

A dollar? I don't understand why Cy needs a dollar to fire me, but I dig a crumpled one out of my pocket and throw it on top of one of the piles on his desk. I could have straightened it for him, but why bother if I'm getting fired.

Cy makes a big show of taking the dollar and smoothing it out before putting it in the chest pocket of his cotton short-sleeved shirt. He leans over and pulls an odd-shaped envelope out of his whiskey drawers and places it on the pile of papers closest to me.

"Open it, kid." Cy leans back and locks his fingers behind his neck to watch.

My pink slip? I square my shoulders and sit up higher in my chair. I'm sixteen now, I've just successfully passed my driver's test earlier this week, and I'm going to take my firing like a man.

"Yes, sir." I don't think I've called my boss that since the interview, but it seems fitting to end the same way I started. Opening the envelope and staring blankly at the paper inside, it doesn't look like what I imagine a pink slip will. It isn't pink, for one thing, and it looks more like a car title. I look closer. Yeah, it's a title to Her Highness, listing Cyrus Lavern Hanover as the owner.

I have no idea what this has to do with me getting fired. To heck with being mature.

"Nice middle name. And here, I always thought *La Vern* was a girl's name."

Cy's head pops up at my rudeness, the hands come down, and he leans forward.

"It's *Lavern,* one word. It's a family name. My mother's maiden name, in fact," he says dryly, "I believe you said derogatory comments regarding one's mothers would result in a duel, if I recall correctly?"

Oops. Cy's sensitive about his middle name. I jump back when he reaches forward to turn the title over.

"Read the name."

"Cyrus Lav…" I begin.

"The other one below it."

"Martin Joseph Jamison. What is this?" My bewilderment is evidenced by the way my voice goes up and cracks on the last word.

Cy grins his familiar grimace. "That, young man, is the title to the car you just bought from me for a dollar bill. You now own Her Highness."

"What?" I can barely form my words. "You're giving me your car?"

Cy leans back in his chair, a self-satisfied grin on his face. "Nope. Sold it to you for a dollar. A real man don't expect something like that car for free. Take good care of her."

"But what will you drive if you don't have Her Highness?

"Don't you worry. I've got one of them fancy new luxury sedans waiting for me down at the dealer. It finally came in this morning and I just need to go in and pick it up. It's bright red and practically drives itself." He beams that kind of smile that threatens to crack his face.

I have a car. I have my own car! I jump up and run to the window, almost knocking Cy over in my zeal to see Her Highness in all of her full *owned-by-me* glory. She's basically free, old enough I can afford her insurance, big enough for some serious parking with Kayla, and okay, well, it'll take a lot of gas to drive her, but she's all mine.

I can barely contain my excitement, until I remember that now I will have a car and my brother won't. With all that Max has been through this year, it hardly seems fair. Once again, I'm the luckier twin.

"Marty, it's not yours until you sign on the dotted line."

I sit, but make no attempt to pick up one of the pens littering the piles of paper on the desk.

Cy waits expectantly and when I do nothing, lets out a huffing sound, and shakes his finger at me. "I know what that look is. Your mom and Max said you'd react this way. You worried Max will be upset that I am giving you a car and he isn't getting one too, aren't you?"

I shrug. Man, am I that transparent to everyone?

"Well, I already talked with you mother and Max about this. He wants you to have the car. Your mother says it will be easier for her to find the money for Max to drive something if you already have a car."

I began, "I really do appreciate the…" but stopped talking when Cy began shuffling through the pile of papers on his desk on his left side. He indicates I should take the right. I don't even have to ask what we are looking for when I find a note addressed to me in Max's sloppy handwriting.

Marty,

I'm not mad.

Take the car from Mr. Hanover.

I am just fine with SHOTGUN!

Get it?

Your twin brother,

The note ends with the messy scribble Max always swears says Maxwell James Jamison. I love that Mr. Literal has gone to the trouble of writing a note and signing his full name just in case I'm confused that it's from some other twin brother. That I don't have.

I pick up the pen and sign my name on the appropriate line.

I have a car.

I have to admit I wasn't sure that bringing Jacob here to St. Louis was a good idea. I knew he'd been suffering after Natalee's death. We all were. It didn't help that Shane and I weren't communicating at all afterward. Then Jacob got arrested for the tagging and vandalism. I was afraid he wasn't going to make it if I didn't do something drastic. I left Shane and we moved here to be near my family. Jacob's been happier here.

I'm so glad we went when we did. Mary Jo's told me how the community treated Max when they thought he was involved in the deaths. Of course, Jacob didn't believe the rumors about his friend and I didn't either. We both knew that the boy cares too much about helping others to do what people were saying.

As for the idea that Max Jamison had something to do with Natalee's death...just preposterous. He loved her almost as much as Jacob did.

Robin Peterson

"Principal Morris thinks there won't be any problems this morning, but remember he said to come to the office if anyone tries to bother you," I caution my brother as we walk down the hall of the school toward his locker. We only have a few weeks of school left, but Mom wanted him to come back. Our principal has been so good about trying to make Max feel comfortable enough to come back that I've decided to be kinder about his stutter.

"I know, Marty."

"And Mom is going to be right outside after school to pick you up."

"I remember, Marty," Max snaps, slamming his locker with a bang.

Man, passive Max sure has disappeared.

"I've got the time to walk you to your first class, if you want."

"No!"

"No?" I'm trying to be a good brother and this is how he's going to act toward me?

"You heard me. I don't need your supervision to get to my classes. I'm not a baby or crazy, either, like people say, and I'm sick of everyone treating me like that. Just go back to your smart friends and your girlfriend *Kay-la* and leave me alone." Max slams his locker shut and stomps away leaving me gaping after him.

What a jerk! I want to stomp to my own class when I notice Claire across the hall. She smiles and walks over to me.

"Guess you heard all of that?" I ask, giving up all pretense she hasn't just witnessed our brother-to-brother words.

"I did. But don't worry, I have sisters and we fight too. We already would've been on the floor rolling around, pulling hair and biting," she comforts.

"That sounds more interesting, at least." I joke. If all of Claire's sisters are as cute as she is, Ray would sell tickets for that babe brawl.

"It isn't. Max is a little stressed about being here, huh?"

"Wouldn't you be in his place?" I shift my backpack over to my other shoulder.

"Yeah. You made it nearly a year with people being jerks. He can make it for a few weeks."

"I guess."

"It's hard being the sibling without the actual problem, isn't it?" Claire asks.

I look at her blankly. Does she have a bipolar sister?

"In my family, it was my sister, Rachel, and it was cancer."

"Okay. Is she…" I pause and then lean in toward Claire. I'm not sure how to politely ask if her sister is dead.

"It's okay. She's fine now." Claire reaches out and pats me on the arm. "Rachel lives in Chicago and interns at one of the big museums."

"That's how come you and Miss Brandel talk about Chicago so much."

"My family goes up to visit Rachel sometimes. It's a lot of fun. You should go sometime." Claire face is bright and shows me that she must enjoy her own visits there.

"Sounds like a good place to plan to see someday, but my family doesn't travel much." Too expensive with all of Max's meds to pay for. Insurance never covers everything.

The five-minute warning bells rings and the hallway is filling up with other students. I point to one of benches in the window alcoves that are set back enough to allow us to speak without yelling or being run over by our classmates. We sit down, our book bags at our feet.

"Marty, I've felt really bad for you these last months. All of the drama. I've been wanting to tell you that I know what's it's like to have someone in the family need medical supervision. You end up feeling like you're just there to help and you're problems aren't as important, right?" This girl is good.

"I understand that Max being bipolar is something he can't control, but it seems like it takes over the whole family." My face heats up, because I never talk about my feelings like this to anyone.

"I know how that is. That was probably true for a couple of years when Rachel was the sickest," Claire says. "But she got better and our family went back to normal. Mom and Dad still call and check on Rachel more often than the rest of us, but she's living her own life."

"That's good, but bipolar doesn't go away. I don't know if I'll ever be free from taking care of Max, or that my Mom will be, either." I let my breath out, shocked that I've just admitted my biggest fear—that I will always be my brother's keeper.

"Maybe, instead of you being afraid that you and your mom will have to take care of him forever, Max is more afraid he won't be free from either of you."

I open my mouth to protest that she doesn't know my brother or his situation.

"Sorry, I just want to help." Claire's face turns red. "I hate to see you upset."

"It's okay. I should take advice wherever I can get it." I smile at Claire. "Go ahead. Give me your best stuff."

"Okay." Claire's eyes light up now that she knows I'm not upset with her. "Max has a regular doctor that supervises his care, right?"

I nod.

"Does he follow what the doctor tells him to do without fighting it?"

That is one thing I don't think we'll ever have to worry about with Max. He isn't willing to take the risks Dad did.

"Yes, but…" I don't know how to explain that Mom and I still worry.

"Aren't a lot of people who are bipolar capable of having regular lives with jobs and getting married with, kids and stuff?" Claire asks.

I nod again.

"I think he might feel kind of boxed in from everyone trying to take care of him. My sister did after the initial difficult part of her illness. We all had a hard time letting go, so she could try to do things on her own."

"But Max doesn't get to stop being bipolar. There's no remission or cure."

"Marty, I'm not sure that my sister would say she ever gets to stop worrying about cancer, either. She's better and she's moved on, but I think it's always there in the back of everyone's mind. " Claire grabs on tighter to my arm. "I think what Rachel fears most is our family seeing her as a burden—not as someone who gives to the family, too. Do you ever let Max help you or show him that you believe he's capable of doing things on his own? Or do you and your mom always try to do everything for him?"

Is Claire right? Do we protect Max too much? Not when it's important to protect him, like when everyone thought he was the Floating Angels Murderer, but in normal everyday situations? I remember how hard Max had to fight to get to stay with Thor the morning he was poisoned, and I realize it's true. Mom and I have made my twin feel useless, when the truth is that he isn't. *Incapable* would be the appropriate college prep word, and it doesn't fairly describe him. No wonder he's angry.

"Claire, I think you may be a genius." I reach over and put my arms around her for a quick hug.

Claire is blushing when I lean back, my arms still around her.

"Actually, I am." She smiles. "I've been tested."

"Me too." Well, it's true.

We laugh and I give her another quick squeeze and this time she hugs me back. We're still laughing when we break apart and stand up, grabbing our backpacks to go to our first classes.

That's when I notice Kayla standing across the hall. Her face is white with rage. I glance down at Claire and realize what my girlfriend must have seen.

"Kayla, I …" I step toward her, but she turns and runs down the hall.

Guess who's not laughing now.

It's midday on Saturday when I stop by the house to change my shirt. I'm between events on my schedule of places to take photos today. It's surprisingly warm for the second week of May. After a morning of shooting the action at the local T-ball games, it's embarrassing to admit, but I stink. I plan to wash up quickly, slap on some cologne and deodorant, and head over to this month's meeting of the library board.

I didn't see Mom's car. Max must be home, because Thor barks a greeting when I come in the back door. At least he's not in the doghouse, where I've been the past couple of weeks with Kayla. She wouldn't even talk to me at all last week, and it's taken a lot of talking and more than a little begging on my part to get her to agree to go out with me later tonight. I want this day to be over so I can work on getting Kayla and I back to where we were before.

I check the time on my phone and there's no time for lunch, so I grab an apple out of the bowl on the island and head back to the bedroom where I can hear Max's voice. Either he's got company or he's saying stuff to the game system again. We both say lots of things to it, when we aren't winning. Some of these things will make our mom threaten to wash our mouths out with soap, if she hears them.

Entering the hall, I can see Max. I am wrong. Max is sitting on his bed talking on his phone.

"...3895 Maple Drive. Thanks. You too. Bye." Max finishes writing on one of those little notepads Mom keeps around the house, before ripping the sheet out and shoving it in his pocket. He jumps when he notices me.

"Hey bro, what's up?" I ask before biting into my apple.

"Huh." Max grunts, a clear sign he isn't in the mood to talk.

I hold the apple with my teeth to free my hands and start digging through my dresser drawer to find a shirt. I find a possible candidate for clean status, take a big bite out of the apple, and slid it over to one hand. With the other I hold the shirt up for the sniff test.

Sniff. Sniff.

Fresh and good to go.

Max blurts, "I need to borrow your car."

"Can't." *Chomp. Chomp.* "I'm working." *Chomp.* "Just stopped by to change..." *Chomp. Chomp. Chomp.* "My shirt. Got a date with Kayla later, too."

"Kayla?" Max sounds disgusted.

Maybe his call had been to a girl and it hadn't gone well. Max has been really moody the past couple of weeks, even for him. I'd thought people at school were being mean to him, but maybe it's just problems with a girl. I knew all about that, these days.

"I need your car. Now." Max insists. "Mom said she'll be back from the store. You can borrow hers."

"So can you." I say jokingly and toss my apple core into the trashcan in the corner. Score! I pull my stinky shirt off and shoot it toward the laundry basket by the closet. Airball! Oh well, I'll pick it up later.

"No, I can't! Just listen to *me* for once, Marty."

"What's that supposed to mean? I listen to you all the time."

Max stands and I can tell he is upset, but I'm not going to roll over and have him be a jerk without some attitude back on my part.

Max glowers at me and punches his fist into his other hand. Hard.

Wow, he really is upset. His face is red and his whole body shakes, and now he's clenching and unclenching his fists over and over. Maybe I should try the nice route.

"Where are you going, anyway? If it's on the way, I can give you a ride."

"I don't want a ride. I said I need your car!" Max yells. "It wouldn't hurt you to share *something* with me. You're the twin who has it all."

Really. Really! A rage I haven't even realized I hold in comes rushing over me, and suddenly Max isn't the only one with a red face and clenched fists.

"What do I have, Max? Because I share *everything* with you all the time. It's hardly ever what I want or need. Here or at school or anywhere." I jerk my clean shirt over my head. My hair's probably sticking up, but I'm too mad to look. "And I have to take care of you all the time, too. It's always, 'poor Max. Shh, let him sleep. Let's not upset your brother. He can't help being so moody. He's sick. Poor Laxy Maxy!'"

Max springs forward until he's right in my face. "You think it is easy to be bipolar? You think I like having you and Mom and everyone else having to take care of me all the time?" He punctuates these questions with shoves to my chest. "You think I enjoyed everyone in this stupid town going around thinking I kill little girls? Being shut up in my room, so people won't try to hurt me or you guys when they see us together? All because I'm the one with a mental illness? Because everyone knows Max is the *Cr...aaa... zzz...yyy* twin. Hey everybody, let's see how long it takes Max Jamison to off himself like his crazy old man did. Isn't that what you think, Perfect Smarty Marty? Isn't it?"

I raise my fists to hit him when he suddenly steps back, breathing hard. It takes everything in me to stop myself from hitting him anyway. Everything. But then I look into the face so much like mine and see more than just anger. There's plain, deep despair.

This is Max. My twin. My brother. The guy who always tries not to hurt others. The person who I know loves me and Mom and Thor more than anything or anyone else in the world. The person I love.

Something is wrong here. Really wrong.

Max puts his hands down and backs away from me, body quivering, gasping for air, and looking down at the floor where Thor is waiting nervously to find out why we're shouting.

"Max, what is it?"

He shakes his head back and forth, left to right, while still staring down at the floor.

I ask the only question I can think to ask. "Max, is it your meds? Are they causing you to act this way?"

Max looks up at me. After a minute he smiles bitterly. "Not this time, Marty. It's not me just acting a little crazy. I wish it was that simple." Max takes a deep breath and shakes his head back and forth. "I'm so sorry, Marty. This time it's something much, much worse."

Max turns, steps over Thor without petting him as usual, and walks quickly down the hall, across the kitchen, and out the back door.

Thor looks up at me like he's asking for an explanation of what has gone on here.

I have nothing.

It's been awhile since I have been able to help someone. Sometimes I think I will just stop, but then someone reminds me that you can't count on people.

I've got a good one to help in mind. On the outside, her life looks like it perfect, but it can't be. Nobody's life really is. I know I'll be able to help her.

Just like I did all the others.

The Killer

32

Ding-dong. I push the doorbell on Cindy and Kayla's side of the duplex again. No answer. I can see her mom's car in the driveway, so maybe they're next door. She said she was babysitting today, but I'm hoping she's already back. I really need to talk to her in person.

I need to cancel our date tonight, and I'm already on thin ice. I wipe sweat off my brow as I head over to try Susan's door. Man, it's hot.

After I ring the doorbell, I think about the reason why I'm trying to break the date. It's Max. Our argument earlier has me worried. I said some horrible things to him and I'm worried how he's going to feel about having the person closest to him treat him like that. I can tell something is not right with him, and I can't figure why he just won't tell me what it is. I tried to call him a few times on the way over here, but his phone just goes to voicemail.

I know I can't take back what I said, but I can try to be a better brother. I plan to stay at home with him tonight and offer him some support. If I do that instead of trying to take over like Claire says, he might tell me what's wrong. Maybe Mom will order pizza and we can play video games or watch a movie together.

"I told Cindy I thought I heard someone at her door. Come on in and let me get you a glass of tea. You look like you're about to melt." Susan opens the front door wider and I gratefully enter the cool house.

Thirty minutes later, I'm still inside drinking tea and eating an appalling amount of cookies.

"Now this one is of Cindy and me after we won the three-legged race at our family reunion." Susan shoves a small, old-fashioned Polaroid photo at me.

"We only won because Grandpa Forrest tripped our bigger cousins on purpose, so we could win," Cindy confides.

"True, but he always said he liked his girls best," Susan confirms and both of them giggle.

I take another swallow of the sweet iced tea they've given me while I wait for Kayla. She's late from babysitting for the doctor who owns the bowling alley. I'd tried calling her before, but Cindy explained that the parents ask her not to have her cell on while she's babysitting. They feel it would be a distraction. Since the doctor's wife is supposed to be giving her a ride home, I've been sitting at the kitchen table with Susan and Cindy while they are sorting old family photos to make new albums. I've seen some great ones of Kayla when she was younger.

"Here's another one of Kayla and Krista together on Valentine's Day." Cindy hands it over for me to see. They both had been cute little girls in their white shirts with big red hearts on the fronts that said, *Be Mine*.

"That's nice." I grin. "I see you and Mom love to put your kids in matching clothes. I think she would still do it if Max and I would let her." I mentally shudder remembering all of the times Max and I wore the same type of outfits until we finally balked.

Cindy throws up her hands, "Guilty. I loved dressing my girls alike. Shirts, pants, dresses, socks, shoes, and even the huge hair ribbons. They loved it. Krista wanted to be just like her big sister, Kayla."

Susan smiles, "She's the one who taught Kayla how to make all those bows she had the kids make for crafts at the activity center last summer."

"Guilty, again." Cindy laughs.

It's nice to see Cindy so relaxed and happy. I study her face and even though I can still see the signs of her battle against alcoholism in the lines on her face, she seems to be doing better. Kayla's told me that the doctors at the last rehab facility think that Cindy's most recent and longer stay might make the difference in her long run recovery. I hope so. She and Kayla both deserve to be happy.

I look up at the clock above the door to the kitchen. If I'm going to try and make Max happier, I need to be going.

"Thank you for the tea. Could you have Kayla call me, when she gets here?"

I already explained to Cindy and Susan I'm breaking our date tonight, with the excuse that Max is having a rough day. I didn't explain that I'm a big reason why it's that way.

"Sure, Marty. It's no problem," Susan says.

Cindy picks up another photo of her girls. "I really thought you were going to stop by to see her when you called to get the address for the doctor's house earlier."

I'm almost to the door when I realize what Cindy said.

I didn't talk to her on the phone today. But I know who did.

I turn around. "You know, I think I might run by and see if I can talk with Kayla before she catches her ride back here. I don't want her to be upset. What did you say the address was again?"

"Here Susan, write it down for him on your pad. It's 3895 Maple…"

I'm out the door as soon as she finishes. I don't know what Max is up to, but I'm on my way to find out.

Call came into dispatch at 5:36 p.m. from a Mrs. Becky Carstairs, resident of 3897 Maple Drive. Said that a young male came to her door, yelling at her to call 911 for an emergency next door at the doctor's place, and then ran off.

I wish I could say it was a total surprise what we found out back of the main house, but it wasn't. We knew who had the access to girls, but we dismissed this one too quickly.

We about messed this one up, but good.

Harold "Chet" Hawkins-Madison Police Chief

33

I pound on the heavy carved wooden door. I peek in again through the sheer curtains covering the long vertical window that is next to the front door. I thought about just trying to open the door and yelling inside, but there's one of those notifications by the steps warning that the premises are protected by some security system. This house looks so expensive, I figure there really is one, and the owners aren't just trying to fake out thieves.

I pull out the paper I grabbed from Susan and check again to make certain I'm at the right house. The big engraved sign, states this is 3895 Maple St., home of the Yandles, Robert, Lena, Olivia, and Aiden. Nobody seems to be inside, so I must have missed Kayla and her ride somewhere in between here and the duplexes. I'll call her later when I get home.

First I want to know why Max called Cindy pretending to be me and got this address. Kayla's mom has talked to me on the phone too many times to be fooled by anyone, except him.

I step down off the massive front porch and start back to Her Highness, looking around at the grounds. This definitely is the richest neighborhood I've ever seen in

Madison. I pull my phone out and try my brother again. I thought Max and I mowed some big lawns over at the lake houses, but this place qualified as an estate. It would have taken me a week to weed eat all of the shrubs that lined both sides of the driveway. I shake my head at the luck of some people and reach into my pocket to pull out my cell and try Max one more time. I want to make sure he's made it home or if I need to drive around looking for him. He'd been gone when I'd come out of the house after our fight, and hadn't answered his phone earlier when I tried.

I tap Max's name on my cell phone and open the door of the car and then shut it again abruptly as my heart sinks to my feet.

Trillll. Trilll.

Max's phone. Close.

I look around and walk toward the sound.

Trillll. Trilll.

Here it is. Max's phone's behind a sculptured bush, hidden next to his old bicycle.

Oh man. Where is he? What's he up to now? Nobody seems to be in the house, so not there. I didn't see him on the vast front lawn anywhere. Back yard, maybe? I walk toward the tall fence separating the back of the property from the front. Gate? Locked. I look around for something to help boost me over and find a decorative rock about the right height. I climb up, jump over, and hope the Yandles don't believe in having guard dogs in addition to alarms.

I land face first into the rough surface of a really big sand box. Great, I'm hot, sweaty, and now covered in gritty sand. I'm going to kill Max when I find him. I brush myself off and hurry to the first building. I peek in the window. Garage. I sneak to the next one and jump up and look inside this one too. Lawn equipment shed. Figures. Then I turn to look into the only building I haven't investigated. Gym maybe?

I hear the scream when I'm a few feet away. As hot as it is outside, I still break into a run and jerk the door open, where nothing can prepare me for the muggy hell on earth I find inside.

Max, Kayla, and a little girl I assume is Olivia, thrash violently in the water. All three of them appear to be bleeding. Kayla and Max have the girl between them and are jerking her back and forth, struggling to gain control of her unconscious body.

At first I'm so dumfounded at what I see that all I can think is how the three of them look like a video I saw of crocodiles thrashing around a young gazelle in the water. Olivia looks just like the bleeding gazelle right before it was torn in two.

Neither Kayla nor Max noticed me as I run forward to the pool's edge. They're too busy fighting for control of the girl as they roll in the water.

They bob up.

"Let her go, Max!" Kayla screams and slaps at Max's hands.

"No, you let her go!" Max yells. I am stunned when he rears back and punches Kayla in the face. What? We don't hit girls. Ever. He isn't going to hit my girl!

I run, screaming at Max, around the pool toward the other side when the group is now. Just as I stick my foot into toward the water to jump in, they come roaring up. I suddenly remember one of the water safety tips from an article I wrote that says to stay out of the water when someone is thrashing about. It didn't cover trying to hurt someone, but I stop and charge farther down the pool's deck trying to grab at someone as they go by. I know if I jump in, it will make the situation worse and somebody will probably drown.

Both Kayla and Max punch at each other now and my brother pulls her ponytail. She uses her teeth to try to bite his shoulder.

"Stop it, Max!" I yell. "Stop it! Don't hurt her." I don't know if I mean Kayla or the little girl, but it doesn't matter since they're beneath the water's surface again.

I look around desperately for something, anything that I can use to break everyone apart. It's then that I notice a large, bloody decorative oar lying a few feet away on the decking next to one of Max's shoes. What did he do?

I hear my brother and girlfriend's heaves for air when they surface again and I grab the oar. Max and Kayla still swing at each other.

"Max, quit it. Quit it!"

Max looks up just for a second at me and Kayla takes this opportunity to drag her nails across his face. I slap the oar on the water. They ignore the slap and my yelling.

I check Olivia's condition. The little girl's head gushes out more blood. It runs into the water in huge red ribbons like the one on her head that flops back and forth wildly as she goes in and out of the water.

"You've got to stop. You guys are killing her. You're killing each other."

It's quiet now. They're all under water. I run around the pool tracking their progress under the pool's surface. Maybe I can get the oar in between them when they come up and force them part. Then I could jump in and control Max while Kayla helps the little girl. That might work, right?

When their heads pop up this time, they're close to the edge and I'm ready. I shove the oar between their faces.

Kayla chokes out, "Help me, Marty. Max's trying to kill Olivia!"

"I am not!"

Kayla knocks the oar out of the way and they disappear for a second or two, but come up almost immediately. I try to get the oar between them again. Blood's running off everyone, leaving even more ribbons of blood in the water. It starts coming off me too when their thrashing shoves the oar into my face. I see stars, but keep on my feet and try to keep up with their progress underwater.

Up they come. Kayla rasps out, "It's Max. He's the Floating Angels Killer!"

Max punches Kayla on the side of her head, hard. "No I'm not. It's her. Kayla's the killer!"

And down they go again.

One of them was the serial killer? Not Rudy Coleman?

I can't figure it out, but I've got to stop this fighting. This little girl's going to drown if she hasn't already. Max and Kayla are going to drown too if this doesn't stop.

I need to think, and I stand staring at the oar the next time they came up.

Somebody must have hit the little girl to make that gash. But which one?

One of them must have hit the girl with this oar. Which one?

Max is the obvious choice, but how can I believe that my own twin, my mirror image, is capable of killing this little girl? Of killing the other?

Kayla is my girlfriend. How could she have done it? I love her. But I love Max too.

Which one?

Think Marty, think. Cy says serial killers have patterns. Find the pattern and you'll find the killer.

I think about what Max and Kayla have in common while I run around the pool's edge to where they should come up next.

I picture imaginary lists on the pool deck.

<u>Both</u>

Worked at the activity center.

Had access to the drowning sites.

Are proving they're strong enough to drown the little girl.

<u>Evidence.</u>

Shoe print. Too small for Max's foot, but police didn't really establish it was really the killer's footprint.

Victims hadn't appeared to struggle. Shows they knew them, but still doesn't help.

<u>Clothing.</u>

Pants, shirts, underwear, socks, hair ties, jewelry.

I just don't know.

I peer down into the water and wish I could see more clearly. I picture Olivia's clothes and hair and her bleeding face. Is there something there that ties this girl to Max? To Kayla?

Yes.

Suddenly I know what to look for when Kayla, Max and Olivia break the surface this time. I tighten my grasp on the oar, swing it back, and prepare to hit and possibly kill either my twin brother, or the girl I love.

This time, I'm the one who's fighting to breathe when their heads emerge from the water. I'm the one waiting until Kayla and Max fight their way closer to the pool's edge. I'm the one who looks at the three of them and sees what it takes for me to know a killer.

And I'm the one whose tears fall on the pool decking, when I make my choice, rear back, and swing the oar. *Crack!*

"I am here with junior, Raymond O'Rear, a member of the student body of Madison High School, as several of them gather here to drape a very special banner across the back of their beloved mascot, Monty the Mule. Raymond, could you explain for our viewers the special meaning of the multicolored ribbons decorating the banner."

"Call me Ray Man. All you hot ladies, just call me. Sorry. Uh, these ribbons show each of the little girls who died in the Floating Angels Murders. The ones from our town. We want everybody to know we won't forget them. We all felt bad that one of our students was, you know...doing it."

"Thank you, Raymond. I understand you are friends with the young people responsible for solving these murders."

"Yeah. I'm really proud of them. We all are, right guys?"

"Okay, well thank you. Could you please remind the viewers of their names?"

"Sure. One of them is Marty Jamison and the other one is..."

Cassandra de Laurens-Reporter

34

"Marty, hurry up with your camera. I want to get this picture taken, so I can get to work. I don't want you to be late on the first day of your junior year."

"Okay, Mom."

I pick up the old camera bag that had been Dad's. The man I used to think didn't appreciate his family enough to live for them. The man that I now realize simply had a medical disorder he couldn't manage. The father that I'm working on accepting and forgiving.

Those two concepts—*acceptance* and *forgiveness*—have been the primary focus of the counseling sessions I've been attending all summer since that evening at the Yandles' pool house.

On the way out the front of the house to meet mom, I stop at the pantry and throw some snacks into the outside pocket of my camera bag. I've gained a couple of inches in height this summer and I'm hungry all the time now. I know I'll be starving before lunch.

It's already humid and warm when I open the front door. Thor waits at Mom's feet, panting. My mother's fanning herself with a large leaf from some bush, trying to stay cool in the August heat. I hand over the camera and remind her which button to push. Then I take my position for the annual *First Day of School* photo. With all the things that happened last year, I had hopes she'd want to skip it. Nope. Mom picks up the camera and points it at me. This year's photo is going to be a little different.

I turn and yell, "Hurry up!"

After a moment, Max ambles through the front door. He looks right at me with that same half-asleep smile he gives me every morning.

And I smile back, happy in knowing I made the right choice that day when I swung the oar and knocked out Kayla, the true Floating Angels Murders serial killer.

What will make this year's photo so different is that it will show two young men who got the chance to be heroes that day in the pool house. Together, we stopped a serial killer and saved a little girl's life.

The ribbons in the little girl's hair and on Kayla's ponytail were the key to identifying the killer. Some of the girls weren't still wearing the bows when they were found, so the police didn't see the pattern. I don't think I would've realized it either, if I hadn't seen pictures of Kayla and her little sister Krista and known of the importance of the hair bows as a symbol of their sisterly bond.

Max is the true hero. He became suspicious that Kayla might be the killer when she said something about caring for people at our birthday party. The day below the quarry, he was so busy looking for the phone that he wasn't paying much attention to anything around him. Now he thinks he must have overheard Kayla say something similar as she took the little girl up the service road. We now know Kayla wore my purple hoodie on that afternoon at the quarry and again at the birthday party. Somehow the combination of those two elements clicked something in Max's head.

So why Max didn't go to the police then? That's simple: he had no real evidence. He had a suspicion, a feeling, and a belief. But society, his friends, and yes, even his family had bullied him into believing that having a mental illness meant his mind wasn't as good or reliable or trustworthy as other people's.

Even the police had little to go on. Other than the clothes that were all water soaked, the only other evidence were prints from Kayla's shoes that day at the quarry. Rudy Coleman had his own set of issues, but what almost got him convicted was the fact that he got Kayla's shoes out of the clothes bin at the activity center after she disposed of them. Since he had access to the victims, a sketchy background, and was wearing the shoes from the crime scene, the police were sure they had their man. That was part of the problem. Although investigators try to be open to the idea of both male and female suspects, there aren't as many women serial killers to begin with and very few teenage ones.

People saw Kayla as normal, because she'd become a master at hiding what she truly felt. Max didn't want to hurt me with his suspicions, so he waited and watched. That's why he saw Kayla strike Olivia Yandle in the head with the oar and throw her body into the pool to drown.

I get asked sometimes what I think made Kayla become a killer. I don't know. I don't think she even knows. The press keeps referring to her as a mercy killer. We all heard her screaming how much she wanted to help the girls as they loaded her into the ambulance. Maybe it's true.

Susan told us Cindy talked about the cause once when she called from her new apartment in the city where Kayla's hospital is located. She said the psychiatrists thought that circumstances of Krista's death, coupled with her father's abandonment of the family, and Cindy's inability to remain sober to take care of Kayla, caused a psychotic break. Although Krista had died from heart failure, she and Kayla were taking a bath together when it began. They think Kayla recreated the scenario in the water, because it allowed her the control to *help* those other little girls escape their own problems. The way that nobody had helped her when she needed it after Krista's death.

The other thing people want to know is how I feel about Kayla now. If I still care about her, knowing what she's done? It still sickens me to know what she did to those little girls and their families. It was even worse when we realized that the Madison girls weren't her first victims. She had killed a couple before, when she and Susan traveled to work sites in the summer.

How I feel about her is something I question myself about every day, and I'm still working on *acceptance* of what she did. I really don't know if *forgiveness* will ever be a part of my vocabulary when it comes to her.

Thor barks and brings my attention back to the picture taking.

"Stand up straight, you two. Now get closer together. I want a shot that shows how much you have grown to send to Nana and Papa." Mom says, doing some barking of her own with her instructions.

Max and I reluctantly assume our traditional picture-taking poses with matching fake smiles. Way too cheesy.

"You two. I'm trying to get a serious picture here." She looks into the viewfinder and pulls the camera back down. She wipes at her eyes. "I'm sorry. Every year I swear I won't. But you two are just so grown up and you still look just alike..

"It's because we are twins, Mom. Remember?" I tease her.

"You should know this, Mom. You had to be there when we were born." Max adds.

I'm about to tell Mr. Literal it's too hot to state the obvious when I see him lift his eyebrow and smirk.

"When it comes to kids, TWO are better than one..." Max begins.

I grin evilly and chime in with him right on cue.

"TOGETHER! Forever."

"Will you two stop saying that!" Mom demands and laughs as she holds the camera up.

"But Mom!" We chorus in perfect sync.

"I swear you two are mirror images of each other in more than one way."

Max and I smile.

Click.

There are worse things to be.

G. A. Edwards

Excerpt from Madison Murders - Book 2
EXPLOSIVE CHARGES

"Murderers!"

"Baby killers!"

"Someone needs to blow up all ya'll."

It says a lot about the last few months of my life, that I barely even look up from the mailbox at the end of our drive to acknowledge this latest pickup truck full of the Younger family haters. No fist raised in defiance, emphatic presentation of a single finger salute, or handful of gravel thrown in anger by this Cord Younger. No sir, all these good old boys will see me do with my hand is wipe my sweaty face and reach in the box to gather up today's collection of hate mail and medical bills for my brother Chase.

It's no secret that the local people of the area surrounding Madison, Missouri, want to drive my family away from the farm that has been owned by the Younger family since the early 1900's. It's been suggested by more than one member of the community that we need to pack up, sell out, and go someplace else for a fresh start. Those are the suggestions we get from the people we call our *friends*.

Others find less direct ways to convince us to go. They employ methods such as weekend potshots at the windows of our hundred-year-old two-story house, contributions of mutilated animal carcasses decorating our fence posts, and additions of sugar to enhance our tractor's diesel tank.

After all, what can we say to convince these good people of our community that they are wrong to treat our family this way?

Nothing.

Because everyone knows that we most likely harbored and produced someone capable of murders. Multiple ones. And of disfigurements and missing limbs and yes, even baby killings. Those are multiples too.

I accept this reality and the fact that my life will never be the same after last spring's explosion.

But I realize something else when I turn at the sound of this same truck racing back down the road toward our farm. Once the burning cloth in the bottle of gasoline leaves the truck window and breaks open in the front field, splattering fire across the drying raked hay, I know what I'll never accept. That anybody has the right to take away the home generations of Youngers have worked so hard to build.

I drop the mail, jump the fence, rip my worn T-shirt over my head, and run toward the flames.

I'm a Younger. We don't give anything up without a fight.

CONTACT THE AUTHOR

G. A. Edwards enjoys visiting with readers. If you would like to speak with her or if you are an educator who would like to receive a free supplemental learning packet, look for her at:

http://gaedwards1.wordpress.com/

http://gaedwards-thewriteway.blogspot.com/

https://www.facebook.com/gaedwardsauthor

https://twitter.com/Galiceson

Made in the USA
San Bernardino, CA
29 March 2014